Also By Michael Coorlim

GALVANIC CENTURY
And They Called Her Spider
Maiden Voyage of the Rio Grande
On the Trail of the Scissorman
A Matter of Spirit
The Collected Bartleby and James Adventures
Sky Pirates Over London
The Tower of Babbage
Fine Young Turks
A Gentlewoman's Chronicles
Steampunk Omnibus

A Gentlewoman's Chronicles

Michael Coorlim

Pomoconsumption Press

A GENTLEWOMAN'S CHRONICLES

This is a work of fiction. All characters and events portrayed in this book are fictional, and any resemblance to real people or incidents is purely coincidental. This book, or parts thereof, may not be reproduced in any form without permission.

Copyright © 2012 Michael Coorlim

Cover Art Copyright © Bigstock.com

Published By
Pomoconsumption Press
Chicago, Illinois

All rights reserved.

ISBN: 148128875X
ISBN-13: 978-1481288750

DEDICATION

For all the strong women
I've known and loved

CONTENTS

1   Sky Pirates Over London   1

2   The Tower of Babbage   27

3   Fine Young Turks   71

SKY PIRATES OVER LONDON

Magnesium-white and fire-orange flashes illuminated the fog above the streets of London. Dark shapes drifted through the ochre industrial smog like great birds of prey, drifting past one another before belching forth their dazzling coloured lights. Occasionally the fog around one would clear enough for keen-eyed observers to catch a glimpse of hull or rigging, but true awareness of their nature was reserved for the luminaries up among the clouds.

Captain Newton Mitchel happened to be close enough to see what the situation was, and he wasn't made much happier for it. "Hard to port!"

The midshipman at the helm of the *HMA Brigadine* inexpertly hauled the ship's wheel into a spin, sending the Royal Armada Airship listing, all but stumbling over where the corpse of the previous helmsman lay smoking and dead at the helm's base. Only hours ago they'd been stationed over Gibraltar, and the crew hadn't been cross-trained enough to efficiently replace one-another in the heat of battle.

The hull shuddered as another bolt of energy struck it, thrown effortlessly by their fog-shrouded opponent as it came into view at the fore. Their foe was larger but sleeker than the British airship, a modern commercial design constructed to stay in the air for weeks between ports. A pair of electro-mechanical cannons had been bolt-mounted to its fore, cone-like devices of wire and clockwork covered in flat circular plates capable of drawing forth the essence of the sky itself and focusing that energy into powerful blasts of concussive electric force. Each hit had shaken the *Brigadine's* integrity and killed a sizable number of his crew.

The *Brigadine* drifted in an arc to orient its broadside towards the oncoming vessel.

"All starboard cannons fire!" Captain Mitchel shouted hoarsely into his command tube, his ragged voice transmitted throughout the ship to those crew that yet possessed ears capable of hearing. A vibration ran through the hull as twelve cannons fired simultaneously, their iron payloads soaring towards their oncoming foe. The other ship slipped out of the way with a surprising manoeuvrability for a vessel of its size. The cannons at its fore began to spark and glow ominously, and Mitchel knew that another attack was imminent. "Dive! Dive!" He fancied that he could hear the shuddering impact of at least one of the munitions the *Brigadine* had let fly, and allowed himself the faint hope that he and some of his crew might yet survive. That hope shattered when he saw the second ship closing out of the fog, its cannons already charged and glowing.

"Queen Victoria preserve us," he said, closing his eyes.

Burning chunks of wood rained down upon the darkened streets of London, accompanied by showers of cinder and the smell of burning ozone. A few of the larger pieces smashed through rooftops, and the scattered pedestrians took cover under bridges and thick awnings. Gentlewoman Aldora Fiske stood unfazed with her shopping bags in the street next to her carriage, squinting at the sky through the fog-enshrouded darkness. A large plank landed with a clatter to smoulder at her feet, a quarter of the Royal Armada heraldry visible etched into the charred surface.

"Miss Fiske, please," her driver said, agitation in his voice. "You'd best climb in. The horses won't stave off panic for long."

She watched the other pedestrians running for cover that wouldn't protect them. "Indeed."

Aldora and her fiance Alton Bartleby sat in her parlour on either side of a silver-plated tea service. In most circumstances it would have been inappropriate for the pair to be alone without a chaperon, but special considerations were afforded them due to the length of the engagement. Even so, tongues did wag, and they limited how frequently they were alone together. It was only proper. While some might be tempted to relax their standards of propriety in the privacy of the home, Aldora was dressed in a proper and practical pigeon-breasted blouse, her skirts brushing the floor. The fashion houses of Paris had begun to showcase hemlines that cleared the floor and approach the ankle, but Aldora would never. Not in London.

"I'm afraid I've no cream to offer you, but would you care for some sugar?" Aldora paused mid-pour.

"Yes, please," Alton said. "One lump. They've cut the milk rations again?"

Aldora nodded, scooping a sugar cube into her fiance's cup. "I am afraid so. Dairy products are in short supply. Much of what hasn't been turned to cheese has soured."

"I blame the heat."

"I place the blame on the blockade," Aldora sniffed. "They're the ones preventing shipments into the city. Have you insight into who they are or who they represent?"

"Sadly not. They don't appear to be Luddites, though I'm sure the blaggards cannot help but cheer at the city's predicament. There's no tie to the local criminal element that I've been able to discern, and the multinational trading cartels suffer as much from this as anyone else. I'm afraid we're as stumped as Scotland Yard on this one." As usual Bartleby stood precariously at the height of men's fashion, his sack coat, waistcoat, and trousers coordinated to look tasteful without going all the way to fey. His stiff collar was adorned with a narrow four-in-hand necktie, a soft felt Homburg fedora resting in his lap. His moustache was waxed and casually curled.

"The Kaiser perhaps? Or one of England's other enemies? The Royal Armada Sky-dock was the first facility targeted, was it not?"

"All diplomats have uniformly denied involvement." Alton shook his head. "And James says that the firepower they're employing is well beyond even Prussia's technological prowess. Some form of galvanic cannons, he wagers."

Aldora wrinkled her nose at the mention of her fiancé's partner. "Speaking of Mr. Wainwright, why has he chosen not to grace us with his presence for tea?"

"Back at our home, down in his laboratory." Alton chuckled. "Working, as is his wont. I can attempt to summon him forth should you miss his wit so keenly."

"Heavens no, I'd hate to interrupt his important work."

"That's where we're at. We don't know who's targeting shipments into the city, and aside from some rumours of a drunk in Calais who claims to have been crew aboard one of the airships, mums been the word."

"Have you looked into that rumour?" Aldora sipped her tea.

Alton paled. Further, that is. "Oh, heavens no. Trust me, I'm all for it, but even though the airships seem to be set on targeting shipping rather than passenger lines, there isn't a captain within the city willing to risk passage across the channel. Not for all the coin I could offer, neither by sea nor by air."

"As dire as the situation is?"

"As dire. Parliament's too afraid of getting all the Lords together in one location to come about a plan of action, and the Queen, God bless her, has been ushered off into one of her bunkers. Nobody else has the power to mandate anything."

"They'll have to."

"Eventually, yes. The gentry will not stand the pinch of rationing for long, but things have a ways to go before they get to that point."

"People drop dead from starvation in the streets, Alton!" An octave's change in pitch was as close as Aldora got to raising her voice. "How much more dire do things need to become?"

"The poor, but the poor are always starving, are they not?"

She gave him a frosty glare. "Don't you start playing devil's advocate with me, Alton Bartleby. I'll not stand for it."

"Sorry, darling, force of habit."

Aldora glared at her fiancé, stirring her tea. After a tense moment her face softened and she continued in a sotto voice. "That's what they're actually saying, isn't it? The Lords? And they're not saying it to get a rise, they're saying it as if they believe it."

Bartleby sighed, regarding his cup, and did not respond. The pair sat still in the silence amongst the luxury of the Fiske family parlour.

Eventually Aldora took a sip of her tea. "Mother's been agitating about our nuptials again."

"Oh, splendid," Alton put his cup aside and ran a hand through his hair.

"She enquired just before you arrived, as she left to visit father's grave. Such familial duties always make her somewhat maudlin."

"What did you tell her?"

"I told her I was deferring to your judgement on the matter."

"Thank you ever so much for that."

"You're quite welcome. But to be serious, Alton, we cannot put the matter off indefinitely. People will talk."

Alton sighed and picked up his cup again, stirring it idly. "Yes, well. We've got a goodly amount of time before we need to cross that bridge. Let the gossips wag premature."

"You underestimate the power of the Season's mutterings. And how easily it gets bored."

"Ah." Alton held up a finger. "But I am well aware of how easily distracted Society can be. Let them twitter on about Bartleby the Bachelor."

"I will not have you make me Aldora the Spinster, Mr. Bartleby."

Bartleby looked hurt. "Aldora! I would never put your good name at risk."

"No, you know too well the value of a Fiske to your social portfolio."

"Aldora!"

"I tease, of course—" She offered back a wan smile, pulling the spoon from her tea. Alton's spoon leapt, seemingly of its own accord, from his cup, splattering droplets of tea across the service, to cling to hers with a metallic 'ting'. "Oh my word!"

Alton stared at the crossed spoons. "Aldora! Is this the good silver?"

"No, just the plated nickel—"

Alton was moving in an instant, grabbing Aldora by the elbow and dragging her away. His explosive rise knocked the service aside, bowl of sugar and teapot falling to splash and scatter across the parlour's carpeting.

"Alton, what—"

"Run!" Bartleby pulled his fiancée towards the parlour's tall picture windows. He covered his face as he leapt through the glass, shattering its pane, and Aldora instinctively turned away from the shards flying past her face. She didn't resist his urgency, knowing full well that when Bartleby was spurred to sudden action that he had good reason. For all the man's faults, she trusted him, and trusted his judgement.

They hit the lawn and rolled just as the parlour seemed to explode behind them. The concussive shock pushed them forth, knocking them from the lawn to the drive leading up to the house. Aldora tucked into herself as she landed and rolled back to her feet, skirts falling about her legs into place without flaw, blouse unmarred by the lawn's earth, a ringing in her ears the only sound she could distinguish, the smell of fire in her nostrils. Bartleby's jacket had been torn by the jagged broken glass, the knees of his trousers muddied, hat missing from his head. He cast about briefly for it and moaned, finding it crushed.

Her hearing gradually returned, and Aldora pushed an errant curl back into her coif, returning to a state of perfect impeccable grace. "Alton, what—"

"Something James said to me." Bartleby fiddled with his hat, pushing the dents back out of its felt. "He kept going on about the science of galvanics, and mentioned that the cannons would interfere with the navigational equipment in targeted vessels. Such navigation is magnetic in nature, so when the spoons clung to one another—"

"You knew that a galvanic cannon had targeted the parlour." Aldora's gaze moved from the smoking crater that had been her family's home's parlour to the sky, where a sleek black shape drifted away through the clouds. "Well done, Alton, you've saved both of our lives."

"As you've saved mine often enough in the past."

The pair watched the burning wreckage of Aldora's home in silence. A fire brigade bell began to ring in the distance, and before long a bucket-line started to form.

"This presents an ugly wrinkle to the blockaders, should they have decided to strike at us directly."

"Strike at me, directly," Aldora said. "Other than the Royal Armada Skyport, my home is the sole structure they've targeted."

"Perhaps they were targeting me? I have been investigating the matter."

"No. If you were their focus they'd have waited until you and your partner were together before attacking."

"That's hardly comforting."

"It was hardly meant to be." Aldora fell silent, wondering why these airshipmen had decided to target her, wondering at what the connection could possibly be.

Jack Fowler dreamed.

In his dream he was still transporting goods across the American heartland from the East coast to the West, still an airship pilot with a major shipping firm. He still lived in Boston, was still married to his childhood sweetheart, and still had a girlfriend in Los Angeles. In his dream, his brother was still alive, and Jack was sober more often than not. This was a welcome dream, a familiar dream, and lately he'd been sleeping as much as possible in order to dwell within it.

An outside influence gradually penetrated his dream-state. His name, repeated endlessly, calling to him from beyond the edges of his perception. It was accompanied by a persistent jabbing.

"Whu?" he gasped, sitting up with a snort, blinking at the strange woman in his room.

"Captain Fowler, I presume?" The woman had gone to great lengths to dress down to better suit the environs of east Soho, assembling a carefully working-class ensemble. Her shirtwaist's blouse was high collared and cut like a man's, her hat was wide-brimmed but unadorned by the feathers and ribbons that ladies of society favoured, and her hair was gathered into a simple knot atop her head. Despite this camouflage, Fowler could tell that she was a gentlewoman of breeding. Common clothes could not disguise the tone in the woman's voice, the surety of her posture, or the imperious confidence in her gaze. She held the parasol she'd been poking him with.

"Yeah." Even dressed down her elegance made him acutely aware of the shabby rough-and-tumble nature of his own clothes, denim trousers and a leather jacket over a shirt that hadn't been washed within memory. They fit the disarray of the room he was renting above the pub, empty whiskey bottles strewn about like forgotten failures.

"Captain Fowler, I have been led to believe that you have an airship available for charter."

Before answering he cast about for one of the bottles scattered about his floor — it was never auspicious to conduct business on an empty stomach. The woman nudged it out of his reach with her toe, and he gazed at it, forlorn. "Yeah."

"I am Miss Fiske, and I would like to charter your services, Captain Fowler."

Fowler leaned over, trying to reach the bottle, which remained just out of his grasp. He whimpered as his fingertips just managed to drag across its surface, Miss Fiske watching him like some interesting new species of insect.

Miss Fiske raised her voice. "Captain Fowler, I said I'd like to hire you."

"I heard you." Jack gave up and rolled over onto his back, knocking empty glass bottles to scatter across the floor. "Where did you want to go?"

"I need transport to Calais."

"Calais?" he pulled a cigarette out of his breast pocket and stuck it between his lips. "Across the channel? You know there's a blockade on, right?"

Aldora fixed her gaze on the man. "You were not my first choice in captains, Captain Fowler. None of the others I approached were willing to take the risk."

He chuckled; the possibility of death was far from a deterrent. "Yeah, I'll give it a go." He sat up and coughed sharply, then spat into a bucket. Aldora remained stone-faced. "Won't be cheap, though."

"Money is no object."

"My three favourite words."

"That's four words."

"Good thing you're not hiring me as a tutor, then?" Fowler stood and stretched, giving a loud, drawn-out yawn. "I can be ready to depart this afternoon."

"Will that be enough time to sober up?"

He gave the woman a wry grin. "Now why on earth would I want to do that, Miss Fiske? Blockade running isn't a sober business."

"I don't find that amusing, Captain Fowler. I insist we wait until dark, at the very least. I don't want to be spotted leaving."

"Fine." Fowler rolled his eyes. "Be at the Soho airfield an hour before dawn. Bring the money and whatever luggage you'll need. Will you be requiring return passage?"

"Perhaps." Aldora folded her arms. "It depends on how quickly we find what we're looking for."

"Oh? And what might you be looking for in Calais?"

"Answers, Captain. Answers."

They departed the next day, before the financial centres of the city woke, when the first shift of working men were starting their toils. The steam and smoke from these factories blended with the morning fog to create a cover that the pair hoped would conceal them from the dangerous warships lurking in the skies above. Fowler had greeted Aldora with his lopsided smile and aggressive bravado, but even his voice faded as they edged out over the water. He'd doused the ship's running lights, and his small private airship, the Persephone, slid through the ominous early morning with only the pale grey morning light to guide her.

A dark shape loomed out of the mists above them, crossing broadside. Ominous green lights shown from the portholes in its hull, and dim figures could be seen observing the Persephone. Electrical arcs crackled the length of the lightning cannons mounted to the ship's fore.

"*Stirner*," Aldora read the ship's name off of its hull. "Why does that sound familiar?"

Fowler slowly turned the ship's wheel to angle away from the ship crossing their path. "Sounds German. Suppose they belong to the Kaiser?"

"Supported by him at best," Aldora shuddered. "If the man wanted to start a war he'd just start it." But that wasn't it. *Stirner*. It was a man's name, she knew that much, but she wasn't able to associate it with any face. Not directly, at any rate.

The *Stirner* drifted back off into the industrial fog, letting the Persephone continue on across the channel.

The *Vieil Métis* was a typical dockside Calais tavern. While lacking the desperation of the East End pubs in London, it never-the-less attracted many of the same calibre of rough and dangerous men, sailors all, on leave while waiting for their vessels to take them to London, or northeast to the Danish fish markets, or south to the warmer French ports. The disruption of shipping across the Channel had been terrible for the city and not much better for its taverns; those who tried to make the voyage had died, and few wanted to wait in port for the situation to resolve itself.

The solitude suited Milos just perfectly. He'd told his story several times to the largely unbelieving ears of the tavern's audience, and now just wanted to be left alone with his solitude and his wine. The former he had plenty of, the latter... his coin was running thin, and he could barely afford enough drink to keep the tavern's keeper from throwing him into the streets. He was deeper in his sorrows than in his cups, and failed to notice the Englishwoman approaching until she'd sat down at his table.

He wiped his nose on his sleeve and glanced around at the rest of the empty common room. "Plenty of seats away from my malaise, *bonne dame.*"

"I've not come for the plentiful seating," she said. Her associate, an American, was ordering a drink from the barman. "I've come to hear you speak."

"Speak?" he asked, uncorking his bottle of wine and drinking a few precious drops. "What could I possibly have to say that would be of interest?"

"Want me to persuade him for you?" Captain Fowler, joining them at the table.

"No." The Englishwoman was dressed for the docks, dull coloured clothes, sturdy and serviceable. She spoke French without an accent, but Milos could see the English in her spine, could see the blueness of her blood in the tilt of her face. "Rumour has that you've been telling a tale I'd much like to hear."

"It's not a tale I care to tell anymore."

The man grabbed the bottle away from him. "Spill it, old salt."

"*Non non non!*" he said, reaching for the bottle. "Don't spill it, I haven't much left, and when I am out the taverner will kick me out into the cold!"

The Englishwoman took the bottle from her companion and placed it back in front of Milos. "There's another bottle for you if you tell me your story."

Milos's eyes narrowed. "More than a bottle, perhaps."

"Sir, I do hope you are not implying anything beyond the bounds of propriety."

Milos was quick to hold up his hands. "Non, *belle-fille*! Do not get the wrong idea! I simply can see that what I know is somehow important to you. Surely it is worth more than the price of a bottle of cheap wine!"

"A bottle of wine now, and if your story tells me what I need to know... then, well, I will pay your room and board in the finest of Calais's inns for a week."

"You are too generous, *bonne dame*, and I pray what I tell you is worth your while."

Milos had been enticed into a life of piracy by his boyhood friend, Jacques. The pair enticed a number of like-minded young men into buying into an airship, and they set about preying on shipping and passenger routes throughout Western Europe. Most airships lacked any defencive weaponry, and it was a trivial matter to escape over the nearest border when they ran afoul of any nation's military. The webs of rivalry and alliance made cooperation between states over a matter of simple piracy unlikely, and the crew of the *Libertine* prospered greatly over the next decade.

"Most of the time we'd put the passengers and crew ashore," he said. "Jacques knew that if we started to kill, we would only draw the full attention of the nations of the world. As long as we remained a minor menace, it was not worth the bother to hunt us down, you know? It was more fun to be gentlemen pirates than cutthroats anyway."

"You and I have very different ideas of what the word 'gentleman' means," Aldora said, but bade Milos continue.

One year ago they had captured a passenger liner travelling up the coast of France. The passengers were relieved of their belongings and most were set aground. "There were a few that were important enough to be ransomed off, if their families had the money." One of these men, an Englishman, declined the opportunity for ransom and instead petitioned to join the crew.

"In the air we are a democracy," Milos said. "When at arms, then it is the captain's word that is law. But for matters such as this, the crew had to agree."

The Englishman, who had given his name as Max ("An obvious pseudonym."), was personable enough about the crew so as to gain approval. He became fast friends with the captain, and offered much good advice regarding tactics and practises.

"I did not trust him as easily," Milos recalled. "He had an edge to him. A hard edge. Always pushing for more, and agitating."

"Agitating?" Fowler asked.

"Talking like a socialist," Milos dismissed. "Going on about class, class, class. About how we working men were exploited by the nation-states and the bourgeoisie and such. To talk to pirates of such things! Those of us who had been with the Libertine from the start, we laughed him off, but some of the younger men, full of fire and the spirit of the age, they listened. But what did it matter? Jacques trusted him, and his ideas were good. Within a year we had purchased a second vessel, and Max was working on getting us better cannons."

"This second vessel," Aldora asked. "The *Stirner*?"

"*Stirner? Non.* It was *La Justice*. Why?"

"No reason," Aldora said. "You were saying about cannons?"

"Yes, Max's idea. He was always petitioning a greater use of force, and more of the men were listening. Jacques and I were opposed, of course — greater weapons only means greater temptation to use them — but the men outvoted us. Max made a deal with some American inventor for some sort of lightning cannons. It was shortly after that that he led the mutiny. It was a quick battle... he threw Captain Jacques over the railing one night after dinner, and had those of us loyal to him put to the sword."

"How did you survive?" Fowler asked.

"I was wounded, see?" The ex-pirate lifted his shirt, showing a pattern of healing scarlet wounds on his chest. "Gruesome, non? Max was an excellent swordsman. He'd pierced me seven times before I'd so much as cleared my scabbard."

Aldora peered closely at the pattern, biting her lip, her face going a little grey. "The *Sette-Punti Stella*."

"*Quoi?*"

"I've seen that pattern before," Aldora said, her voice a whisper. "The 'Seven-Point Star.' I've seen that manoeuvre performed."

"It was painful, let me tell you."

"It's a secret technique of the Castgnaga school." Aldora stood.

"Whatever it was, when he had struck me so, I dropped my cutlass and fell to my knees in shock. They threw me over the side, and only the cold salt water revived me. It was my great fortune that a fishing boat found me before I drowned."

"It wasn't shock. The Seven-Point Star targets the nerve clusters of the major muscle groups and induces paralysis. There are only six men alive today who can perform it." She paused. "Five men. Thank you for your tale, Milos. I'll set you up for the week wherever you'd like to stay."

"Merci. This place is as good as any."

Out on the street Aldora turned and handed a parcel to the Captain. "I need you to return with this to London."

"What, you're not heading back with me?"

"No. I'm off to New Jersey, and then New York."

"I don't like the idea of leaving you to your own devices, Miss Fiske." Fowler took the parcel reluctantly.

"Believe me, this is a matter of utmost importance, Captain. I need you to go to my home — what's left of it — and retrieve a package for me from the hope chest in the closet of my sleeping quarters. A bundle of envelopes tied with a blue string. Can you do this for me?"

"Yeah."

"This parcel contains the address in New York that I will need the bundle shipped to, as well as sufficient postage and with the pay you've been promised."

"As you like it, Miss Fiske. Be careful."

"What I need is expedience. I cannot afford careful."

"You are one of the most revolting men I have ever met," the words left Aldora's mouth almost conversationally, as if she were discussing the weather.

"I've no doubt that a woman of your charms has known a great many men," Thomas Edison said with a sneer. "But I am afraid that those charms won't avail you here. I'm a happily married man, Miss Fiske—"

"You're an appalling bore."

"—and an honest businessman. Many clients come to me seeking innovation, and these clients appreciate the discretion I provide them with."

Aldora sat across the large Mahogany desk from Edison. Papers littered the desk, some of which were patent applications, others financial documents and ledgers. Thomas Alva Edison himself was in excellent shape for a person of sixty years. His wealth and success had not made a soft man of him.

"These men are pirates of the worst sort, Mr. Edison. They've killed a great many merchant airmen and members of the Royal Armada."

"It's none of my concern what my innovations are used for, I simply care that they work." Edison opened a box on his desk and removed a cigar.

"That's a monstrous indifference!"

He pulled a cigar clip from his pocket. "That's capitalism, Miss Fiske. American ingenuity knows no bounds."

"Not the bounds of decency, that's for certain."

Snip! went the clip, and Edison stuck the cigar in his mouth. "Your bleeding-heart humanism smacks of Communist sympathies, Miss Fiske. Such is the speech of Unionisers and anarchists."

"And you sold powerful galvanic weapons to pirates!"

"Capitalist pirates!" Edison lit his cigar, taking a puff, and blowing a ring of smoke into the air.

"So you condone piracy? I'm surprised, even for you that's a new low."

"I condone the Capitalism. Tell me, Miss Fiske, how do you suppose that the other houses of Europe will respond when they see that one ship armed with Edison Electro-Cannons held the entire British Sky-Armada at bay? I'll be swamped in orders. Drowning in money."

"You're disgusting."

"There's a war coming," Edison was suddenly serious, sitting forward in his desk. "A great war. War like this Earth has never seen. The alliances of old in Europe permit nothing less, Miss Fiske."

"And you intend to profit from it."

"I intend to survive it. America isn't bound by Europe's tangled skein, Miss Fiske. When Europe burns, America will emerge as the greatest nation, untouched by war, an industrial giant to usher in a new era of prosperity and enlightenment."

"Then why do you supply nations with these horrible weapons?"

"Because the more devastated Europe is, the stronger America will be. Galvanic rifles. Resurrected troops. Ironclad airships. Clockwork steam-tanks." Each syllable came out of Edison's mouth a staccato burst. "After the horrors of war, all of Europe will clamour for sane American dominion, and inventors and engineers will lead the way."

"I was wrong," Aldora said bitterly. "You're not a bore. You're a monster."

Edison sat back, blinking, and seemed to recover his composure. "You'll have to forgive me, Miss Fiske. I had no intention to upset you so. For your own good I'm afraid I must cut this interview short."

"Please," Aldora said, leaning forward. "Tell me the name of the man you dealt with. Tell me what he looked like!"

The door to Edison's office opened behind her. A pair of his assistants, large and broad-shouldered men with cruel smiles and scarred hands, stepped inside.

"Good day, Miss Fiske."

Back in her West Orange hotel room Aldora sat and unwrapped the package that Captain Fowler had sent to her from London. Letter after letter, written in the same elegant hand, on the same Parisian stationary, all telling her the same thing. Screaming it so loudly that she couldn't ignore the signs. Her hands trembled as she carefully slid each missive back into its envelope, and she felt faint as she carefully placed them atop her room's desk.

"Grayson," she said in a small, almost childlike voice. "Oh, why, Grayson?"

Her hand drifted almost instinctively to the locket around her neck.

Dark figures moved through the West Orange Farragut Hotel corridors, men with hats pulled low and coat pockets bulging with nefarious intent. If any of the guests or staff saw their silent passage they kept quiet, knowing the man they worked for, and knowing that discretion was the better part of valour. Neither man tarried in their dark task, proceeding swiftly and full of menace up to the hotel's second floor, down to the end of the corridor to the spacious suite occupied by the lone travelling Englishwoman, their shadows contrasting with the yellow patterns of the hall's wallpaper.

Gloved hands used delicate tools to spring the hotel's lock, and the well-maintained door's hinges remained silent as the pair crept inside. Dangerous tools both blunt and sharp were pulled from jacket pockets, and the murderous men descended on the still form beneath silk sheets.

A ripping blade found not soft yielding flesh to part, but rather goose-down-stuffed pillows, and a length of pipe cracked not skull but flexible mattress.

"The hotel management shall be quite displeased," Aldora spoke from the darkness, turning on a lamp to reveal herself in a chair across from the bed, pistol levelled at her would-be murders. "You've made a dreadful mess of their sheets."

The man with the knife growled and took a half-step towards the woman, only to be halted by his partner.

"A dead-shot, this one," he warned.

"She's just a girl," his partner said. "I doubt she could hit either of us."

"Care to wager your life, sir?" Aldora asked.

"I don't," the man with the pipe said. "Look at the way she holds the piece."

"So?"

"Thumb on the hammer, ready to slip. She'd drop us both before we even heard the report."

His partner was silent.

"Go." Aldora gestured towards the door with her free hand, the pistol level on her intruders. "Tell Mr. Edison that I've gotten what I've come for, but that our business is not yet settled. Understand?"

"Damn right we're not done." The knife-wielder growled, but allowed his partner to pull him back through the doorway.

"You're looking well, Nikola."

They both knew that it was a lie, but the inventor smiled anyway. "And you remain as radiant as ever we meet, Aldora. If I'd known you were coming by, I'd have cleaned up for you."

Aldora glanced around the brick interior of the Wardenclyffe Tower's facility building. The entire building was constructed in the style of the Italian Renaissance, and the laboratory area contained all manner of electromechanical devices, few of which she could identify. To Aldora's untrained eye, everything was bulbs and tubes, wires and cables. Through a great window in the back she could see the wood-framed tower itself, almost two-hundred feet tall, with a steel hemisphere cupola at the top.

Nikola Tesla followed her gaze. "Do you like it? Overly phallic, I know, but in a way it could not be anything else. The shaft sinks another hundred meters into the earth."

"Good heavens, why?"

A strange sort of mania flashed briefly though the inventor's face. "To give it such a grip on this earth that the whole of the globe might quiver."

"Nikola," Aldora said softly. She had told him of her visit, both by telegram before leaving France, and again before leaving New Jersey, but he'd been honestly surprised to see her appear at the entrance to his machine shop.

"If I get the funding I need," he continued, turning back to his mass of wires and tubes, "it will be the core of my World Wireless System. Imagine. A world linked through free and abundant energy. There would be no more struggle. No more conflict. No more need for war."

"Edison says that the world will fall into a great war within the next decade."

"Edison!" Nikola spat and raised his fists. "What does he know? He is a reprehensible man. An uneducated man with contempt for book-learning and no interests other than business. Science is just another investment, patents just a revenue stream. What I could have done with his resources..."

Aldora placed a hand on the man's shoulder. "It's been too long, Nikola."

He turned, clutching at her hand like a drowning man. Hers was one of the few touches he had learnt to abide. "It has been how long?"

"A decade, almost."

"A decade?" He turned back to his workbench. "I hear that you're engaged now. Is he a good man?"

"Good enough," Aldora said. "One who will give me the freedoms I require to live the life that I desire."

"Good," Tesla said. "A decade. I suppose I am an old man to you now?"

"You have the energy of a man half your age."

"Energy. Yes. Hm."

He seemed to drift off again, thinking thoughts that Aldora could not begin to fathom. She waited patiently for his attention to return.

"Edison, you said. You have spoken to him?"

"Yes. Of necessity."

A hurt look crossed Nikola's face. "And you did not come to me?"

"Oh Nikola," Aldora said. "No. Edison sold some sort of galvanic cannons to some criminals that are using them to terrorise London, but he wouldn't tell me anything about them."

"London?" Nikola said. "That won't do. London will be important."

"Important?"

Nikola turned and erased a chalkboard alongside his instrument panel. "How long can you stay?"

The question seemed to surprise Aldora. "A few days, I suppose?"

"Three days. I will need three."

"I can stay three."

"*Prvoklasan!*" he exclaimed.

Over the next three days Nikola Tesla built a strange looking generator for Aldora Fiske. It looked like all the rest of his electromechanical apparatus did — wires and tubes — but this device seemed even more slap-dash jury-rigged than the rest of it.

"What does it... erm..." she asked, examining the breadbox-sized device.

"I call it an Ionic Shield," Tesla said. "It will protect you from Edison's galvanic weapons. Or any other electricity-based armament, I suppose."

"Marvellous!"

"It will de-ionise the emissions of the Galvanic Cannons and render their issue inert. This is only a prototype, though. I am afraid it will burn out rather quickly, but it should be enough to get an airship close enough to board the pirate vessel."

"How does it work?" Aldora asked.

"Simply mount it to one of your airship's hard-points. It will function reactively. It's functioning now, in fact, aligning the ions of the surrounding air. Don't worry; normal static electricity will not burn the device out, nor will normal operation of an airship."

"Nikola," Aldora said. "Do you mean to tell me you've developed an anti-lighting field?"

"Oh," he said. "I suppose I have. Perhaps I will patent it, and get rich like that *kopile* Edison."

She leaned forward and gave the inventor a peck on the cheek. "Thank you, Nikola."

He turned and grabbed her hands again. "Be careful, Aldora."

"I will."

"And do not wait another decade to come see me again!"

"I won't! Perhaps I'll invite you to the wedding."

"Pfah," Nikola grinned.

"Why am I doing this again?" Fowler asked, glancing back over his shoulder as he worked to attach the Ionic Shield to *Persephone's* bow. The old barn that the American pilot stored his airship in was littered with spare machine parts and tools largely kept in bins and buckets.

"Money," Aldora said.

"Lots of money," Fowler clarified.

"And the gratitude of London and the United Kingdom," Aldora added.

"Will that gratitude also be monetary?"

"I cannot speak for the Home Office," Aldora said, "but I cannot imagine that being the man who saved London would not result in excellent business contacts."

"Business contacts." Fowler mulled. "I like that. Sounds respectable."

"Oh, it is," Aldora assured.

"Fine. Let's get on with it, then." Fowler stepped down from his stepladder and carelessly tossed his wrench into one of the buckets.

"Is that the American 'Can-Do' attitude I've heard so much about?"

"No," Fowler said, wiping his greasy hands off on a kerchief. "But if you're curious about it and we can push our departure back a bit I can give you a demonstration."

He stepped in close to Aldora, wry grin on his face, his earthy graphite scent filling her nostrils. His proximity was a physical thing, registering on her skin despite the inches between them. Aldora's bemused expression didn't falter. "Alas, Mr. Fowler, I'm spoken for, and we cannot afford even a few minutes' delay."

He turned back towards his airship with a barked laugh. "Well enough, Miss Fiske. Let's get on with this suicide mission of yours."

Luck held with the *Persephone*, and the sleek form of the *Stirner* was swiftly discovered in the fogs above London. The larger airship ignored the smaller vessel until it became clear that the *Persephone* had plotted an intercept course. The fog was lit with an incandescent glow as the pirate's Galvanic Cannon charged, small auras flickering around its generators, a high-pitched whine audible even aboard the smaller vessel.

"Let's hope that your mad scientist's shields work," Fowler said, jaw set.

"I have the utmost faith in Mr. Tesla's work," Aldora said.

Fully charged, the Galvanic Cannons crackled and fired bright white arcs of electric death towards the smaller vessel. It seemed to split as it reached the sphere of invisible ionised air around the *Persephone*, fracturing and cascading to form a jagged net over the border of the shield's protection. It glowed bright white for an instant, almost blinding those within, and the cabin rocked with a slight concussive force, but when it faded Fowler's vessel appeared unharmed.

"It worked!" Fowler said. "Bully for your Tesla."

"We're not aboard yet."

There was a pause aboard the *Persephone*, and the *Stirner* began charging its Cannons again.

"Brace for impact," Fowler warned.

The lightning cannons fired again. This time the arcs came closer to the *Persephone* before they split, and the jagged electric net they dissipated to was markedly smaller, almost touching the *Persephone's* hull. The concussive force that struck the ship was more powerful, sending Fowler sprawling, and slamming Aldora against the hull. The ozone smell of the Ionic Shield had grown more noticeable, and small wisps of smoke began to issue from its innards.

"It'll not protect us from a third hit," Aldora warned.

"All ahead." Fowler pushed the Persephone's throttle to full, and the ship lunged forward.

"Captain Fowler?"

"No time to look for a bay and come in for a soft landing." The Captain stared directly at the *Stirner*, his jaw clenched, eyes narrowed. "Brace for impact!"

Aldora wrapped her arm around a length of hanging chain and set her hip against the railing. The *Stirner's* Cannons began to charge a third time, and through the cabin's forward windows small arcs of electricity could be seen playing over the surface of the ship.

"It's going to be close!" Captain Fowler shouted over the ever-increasing whine of the galvanic weapons.

There was a bright flash as the Ionic Shield, now scarcely larger than the *Persephone's* hull, came into contact with the electrically-charged surface of the *Stirner*, a bright shock-wave that seemed to travel the length of the other ship's hull. The smaller vessel crashed into the hull of the larger, piercing it like a dagger to the heart.

"You've certainly kept me waiting long enough, though I cannot imagine that pirates are known for their promptness."

The handful of men that had been dispatched to see to the crash-site glanced at one another uneasily. They were hard men, anarchists and killers and rogues who would back-stab their best mates for the most trivial of reasons, carrying well-used rifles and sharpened cutlasses, but they seemed unprepared for the sight of Aldora sitting atop the crate in the cargo hold, legs demurely crossed, folded parasol in her lap, dressed in impeccable London fashion, hair perfectly coiffed, examining the disposition of her makeup in a hand mirror among the smoke and flames from the *Persephone's* wreckage.

"Where's the rest of your crew?" one of the pirates demanded, brandishing his cutlass.

"You will take me to your Captain now."

"What we'll do is run you through and toss you out the hole your junk-heap made in our hull!" One of the others sneered, stepping forward. "After having our way with you, perhaps!"

Aldora was on her feet in a flash, body extended in a perfect lunge, parasol extended so that its razor-tip brushed the pirate's throat. "What you shall do is escort me to your captain, or I shall be compelled to hurt you quite badly. I am offering you parley. I suggest you take it."

He stared down at the edge near his throat. "You'd never take all of us. Our riflemen would have you before you'd taken two of us down."

"Perhaps," Aldora said, stance rigid, parasol unwavering, her tone's ice being eclipsed by the fire in her eyes. "But you'll be there first to escort me into hell."

He glanced down at her parasol's tip once more, its edge catching the firelight.

"Aldora?" The Pirate Captain seemed shocked to see her. He was dressed casually, sloppily, in an uncared-for French military airship-captain's jacket. It didn't quite fit him, the man he'd taken it from being slightly broader of shoulder and thicker of waist than the tall and athletic captain. It seemed his sole concession to his station, worn over continental-style working-man's trousers and an unlaced poet-shirt. "I thought I blew you up?"

"Grayson." The pirates had taken her parasol, which she surrendered only after extracting their word that they would take her to their leader, and the assurance that she could kill them just as easily with her bare hands.

He boggled at her a moment longer, then laughed and ran a hand through the unruly hair atop his head. "I should have known! It takes a Fiske to counter a Fiske. Fantastic."

Aldora's tone and expression remained carefully neutral. "What I find fantastic is that you still consider yourself worthy the name, dear brother."

Grayson Fiske scowled, turning away from his sister to gaze out through the London fog. "I do not consider the name worthy in the slightest. Just another wealthy family feeding from the blood and sweat of the working class. The Fiske name is as worthless as any other; I've cast it aside and taken a new one."

"Stirner."

"My favoured philosopher." Grayson cracked a smile. "You remember from my letters. Maxwell Stirner's egoism has become the guiding light in my life."

"I remember your arrogance and anticipated that you'd name your flagship after yourself."

Grayson's smile twitched and faded. "We never used to bicker so."

"You didn't used to kill people. And piracy?"

"Propaganda of the Deed," Grayson said. "What the Stirner does is send a message, Aldora."

"The only message I see is a criminal one."

"And?" Grayson asked. "Criminality is as valid a lifestyle as that of the upper classes, perhaps less exploitive, and certainly less deceptive about it."

"My brother, the petty thug."

"There's nothing petty about it, dear sister. Our piracy is a personal and violent rejection of an intolerable society. More-so, it's an example to the oppressed. They needn't follow the rules set by their social betters to entrench their own position."

"My brother, the economic terrorist."

Grayson half-turned towards his sister. "I don't think I care for your tone."

Aldora's tone remained lightly mocking. "I don't think I care for your hypocrisy. You claim you desire to encourage the working man to rise up and cast off his shackles? Who do you think your blockade is hurting more? The wealthy bankers might need to ration the sugar for their tea, but the poor are starving. Do you imagine that they'll thank you before they fall dead in the streets? Do you suppose the last words on their lips will be praise for their selfless pirate benefactor?"

"Sacrifices must be made," Grayson said, crossing the room to glare at his sister. "And the poor are used to suffering, to dying, while the well-off cannot abide the loss of their luxuries. Do you imagine that this rationing is equitable? Of course not. The poor must ever be content with the scraps from the table of the elite. When the situation grows intolerable enough — and it shall — the proletariat will rise and cast the upper class from their pedestals to crash and shatter on the cobblestones of Downing Street."

"I don't think you've thought your cunning plan all the way through."

"You see a flaw?"

"Only the part where you're utterly delusional."

Grayson's face flushed. "I'd hoped that you'd at least understand,

Aldora, after our years of correspondence. You seemed sympathetic."

"Yes, well, I am afraid that it is difficult to convey a proper tone of condescending patronising over an epistolary medium."

Her brother turned violently from her, hand lighting to the hilt of the rapier he wore at his hip. "Where are the rest of your crew?"

"Dead in the crash, I should imagine. Fortunate enough to be spared your ridiculous schoolboy philosophy."

Grayson turned abruptly towards the men he had standing by. "Take her to the brig, and join those looking for her compatriots."

An airship's engine was a complicated thing of gears, steam, and steel. Cogs spun, pistons pistoned, and sprockets... did whatever sprockets did. Fowler wasn't too sure exactly what a sprocket even was, but he wasn't an engineer. The maintenance he performed on the Persephone was limited to checking the oil every so often and tapping at the gauges if they went into their red-zones, whatever that meant. Probably explosions. He paid a mechanic to look the thing over once or twice a year whenever it started making more horrible noises than he could tolerate and they presumably fixed it.

All that was moot, of course. The Persephone was lost. It was a financial loss more than anything; his ship had undergone enough repairs and retrofits since he'd expatriated that he doubted there was a single original rivet left in the heap. Still, a ship was more than its hull and gasbags, it was the intent and memories it held.

No great loss then. If he were lucky, the Home Office would be grateful enough to give him a handsome reward. Or perhaps Ford, Daimler, or Wolseley or one of the other major airship manufacturers would be willing to sponsor a state of the art vessel to the captain that had saved London.

Fowler pondered these thoughts as he stared into the *Stirner's* engines. Somewhere, that English woman was confronting the ship's captain. His role in the plan was to somehow disrupt the ship's operation to cause enough of a distraction so that she could... do something. He wasn't exactly clear on that part, but Miss Fiske seemed confident, and that was enough for Fowler. An airship was a complicated machine, and it took a certain technical hand to make any significant changes.

Musing on his inevitable reward, Fowler picked up a length of pipe and started smashing it into the *Stirner's* exposed engines, the sound of iron on brass and steel echoing throughout the cramped engine room.

The *Stirner* suddenly lurched as one of the engines cut out, and Aldora was tossed into one of the quartet of pirates that was escorting her. The man grabbed her by the elbow to steady her, then his cutlass was in his gut, and she was pulling it free to eviscerate the man on her left. She'd killed three of her guards before the fourth even realised that she'd slipped the rope that had bound her wrists, and he fell back against the wall in fear and surprise.

"It looks like you'll have to go to hell without me," Aldora said, almost apologetically.

If Grayson Fiske was surprised when his sister re-entered his stateroom he did not deign to show it. "It's come to this, has it?"

"It needn't end this way, my dear brother. Surrender yourself to me, and I'll see you get the care you deserve."

"More favouritism?" He sneered and pulled a case of rapiers from the wall. "A commoner's care would be the gallows, and yet the high-born Fiske gets rehabilitation."

"The inequality of a sister for her elder brother. Her only brother." She cast the cutlass she'd taken from the slain pirate to the side, catching one of the rapiers as he tossed it to her. "I have a certain pull with the home office. You don't have to die!"

"We all have to die, dear Aldora. Some of us sooner than others."

Aldora looked down at the rapier in her hand, and when she raised her head the anguish she felt showed clearly on her face. "Please, Grayson. I implore you—"

"I implore you!" He stepped across the room towards her. "Join me, Aldora. Give up the ways of the cultural elite. You think to save me? I offer you the same courtesy. Our family tree was watered with the blood of the common man, and you see nothing wrong with growing fat from the fruits of their labours? I have committed a small evil, but what is it compared to the injustice of the class divide?"

"I am not responsible for the vagrancies of class and culture." The tip of Aldora's rapier slowly raised from the floor as she spoke. "I am not responsible for the injustices of the modern world or those of the past. I am not responsible for the theoretic millions toiling to enrich the few. I am responsible for my family, for my blood, for my brother. My dear, sweet brother, ill of mind, sick of spirit, blind or uncaring to the suffering he causes."

She stood in a rigid en guard stance, blade held horizontal. She flicked the tip towards him. "Come, my brother, and feel the healing caress of my blade. Let me rid you of the privileged blood you so despise."

A half-scowl was the only telegraph of Grayson's assault as he stuck out with a quick lunge towards her heart. She pivoted to the side, letting his blade pass by, then brought her rapier against his to knock it aside. He struck at her again and again in a controlled fury, while she calmly deflected each of his strikes. At the end of his flurry she let herself fall back, catching herself on her free hand, extending her blade out in a passata-soto towards his midsection. He swept the tip of her attack aside, but was caught off guard by the boot heel that kicked his legs out from under him.

Aldora used her braced palm to push herself back up to her feet, using the forward momentum she'd earned to extend herself in a lunge towards her brother. He deflected with his rapier's hand-guard, riposting against the side of her head with its pommel. She recoiled, momentarily stunned, and he pressed the attack with a vicious tip slash meant to take out an eye. She twisted back, rolling over the stateroom's table, but felt the hot pain as the edge of Grayson's rapier sliced through her cheek. A second attack pierced her shoulder, and a red rose bloomed as her blood seeped into her blouse's fabric.

"When we last fought," Grayson said, driving the tip of his rapier towards her throat, "I bested you handily."

"When we last fought," Aldora responded, effortlessly battering his attack aside and pulling the stiletto from her hair, "I was eleven."

The dagger's sharp point found no resistance as she plunged it into his breast, puncturing one of his lungs. He stared down at its pearled hilt as he sat back into one of the stateroom's chairs, so heavily that it fell over backwards. Aldora stood over him, face passive, as he made no effort to get up.

"You killed me," he said. "Mother will be upset."

"I shouldn't think so," Aldora said quietly, watching her brother die. "She gave up on you long before I did."

"I'm sorry."

"I know."

"The crew has escaped in one of the ship's boats," Fowler said. "We should take the other one."

It had been easy enough for Fowler to find the bridge, and by the time he had there were no sign of the tears Aldora had shed for her brother. She stood, arms folded, gazing into the fog. "The other ship will be by presently."

"Other ship?"

"There are two. If we only disable one, I can't say we'll have accomplished much. The other one will come to investigate why this one's fallen still."

"You're bleeding," he pulled a clean kerchief from his jacket pocket, wiping some of the blood from Aldora's cheek. "Let's get you bandaged or your pretty little face is going to scar up."

"It's small. It'll heal fine."

"And your shoulder—"

"I'll heal. I've had worse. But I don't think I can crank the Galvanic Cannon's generator with the injury."

"Okay. Go on and wait in the other ship's airboat. There should be a medical kit there at any rate. After I take care of the other ship, I'll join you and we can get the hell out of here."

She paused for a second, looking down at her brother.

"Bastard caused a lot of trouble, didn't he?"

Her voice came quietly. "I believe he did, Mr. Fowler. I shall await you in the ship's airboat."

Fowler didn't have a long time to wait before the other ship arrived, its name visible on the hull, *La Justice*. "So it was the *Libertine* that you named after yourself, egotistical bastard."

He leaned forward and started turning the hand-crank that charged the Stirner's generators. He'd have to act fast; La Justice would notice his Cannons charging and certainly try to take him out first. As long as he had enough of a lead he'd be able to blow them up before they had a chance to finish charging their own. To his dismay, the crank moved easily, frictionlessly. He turned to the ship's tube that connected with the airboat bay.

"Uh, Miss Fiske? We have a bit of a problem."

"What is the nature of this problem, Mr.Fowler?"

"Well, I think that contact with Tesla's Ionic Shield shorted out Edison's Galvanic Cannons."

There was silence from the other side before Aldora responded. "Very well. Come to the airboat; we'll escape and alert the Home Office. We've still done the city a great service in cutting the pirates' firepower in half. Perhaps what remains of the Royal Armada can fight them off when it arrives from India."

"Like hell," Fowler muttered, turning the ship's wheel to orient towards *La Justice*. "Time for some of that American Know-How."

"Mr. Fowler, what are you doing?"

"Miss Fiske, I'm going to have to insist you take off without me."

"Mr. Fowler, you are not to attempt to ram the other ship! There's been too much loss today for your suicide to present an acceptable option, and —"

Fowler shut the cap on the ship's tube, cutting off Aldora's protests. "Good Lord, you do go on."

He tilted the Stirner, watching out a port window as the ship's airboat slid out the open bay. He then fixed his gaze ahead, watching as someone on La Justice sent a semaphore message.

"Even if I knew what them flags meant, I only got one thing to say to you," he said, pushing the airship's throttle as far as it'd go. "Geronimo."

"It's as if you were never wounded," Alton Bartleby said, tilting Aldora's face by the chin. "Completely healed."

"Fiske's heal quickly," she informed him, pulling away and refreshing her tea.

"Well, if you'd be more careful when riding you'd never have fallen to begin with. Aside from the tumble, how was Calais?"

"It was France. A decent holiday."

"Did you find what you were looking for?"

Aldora considered the question while stirring her tea. "Yes. I rather think I did. What happened with the blockade?"

"Well, word has it that an American pilot took it upon himself to storm the ships himself. He singlehandedly took one of the ships, then used it to ram into the other."

"That certainly sounds American."

"Oh, indeed. It rained flaming debris for the better part of an hour. Not very thought out, American Pilot."

"But he saved a goodly number of lives, Alton."

Alton sniffed. "Hardly in a proper way. But that's the American style, is it not? Anyway, the Home Office is going to build a statue to the brave Captain, possibly give him a posthumous knighthood, and all the broadsheets are running with it."

"I suppose it's what he would have wanted." Aldora sipped her tea. "Americans."

MICHAEL COORLIM

THE TOWER OF BABBAGE

THE TOWER OF BABBAGE

"We may never know precisely what brought Charles Babbage to the jungles of Mexico, why he chose to make the journey into the foreboding Lacandon, why he sought out the ruins of the ancient Mayan people. All we can definitively say is that he travelled from ruin to ruin with a retinue of engineers and craftsmen, examining the remains of ancient clockwork and taking measurements."

Carvel White looked out of place but at ease in his dark single-breasted morning coat, matching black waistcoat, and striped trousers against the backdrop of the tropical stone ruins. He may have been miserably hot in the heavy hanging tweed, but it had become a point of professional pride to the master thespian to avoid complaint. His voice projected the dignity of age but none of its frailties as it echoed across the ancient limestone.

"His last stop was here, at the ruins of *Zipactonal*, where he remained the longest. Babbage spent months here in the jungle, encamped before these very stone steps. When asked about his business here years later, Mr. Babbage merely smiled and said—"

"Cut!" The shout rang out across the ruins. "The girl's in the shot."

"Bloody hell!" Carvel pivoted in place, shading his eyes against the sun, peering up the ruined Mayan pyramid's slope at the young girl scrambling along its decrepit surface. He didn't know if it was typical for these 'film' projects or not, but this had to be, by far, the least professional production he'd ever had the displeasure of taking part in. "Robinson, control your wretched offspring!"

The film crew's overweight director lifted his glasses and wiped the sheen of sweat from his ruddy face. "Don't put yourself out, Mr. White. We'll take up again from the start of your anecdote."

The girl's father, the crew's guide, ran a hand through the back of his shaggy dark hair. Where the crew's jungle khaki's were so new that they were practically still starched, his own outfit was faded and streaked with the mud of dozens of previous expeditions. "Sorry about that, Mr. Girnwood."

"Just keep her off the set, Henry," the director said.

"Penny!" The man cupped his hands, calling up the ruins to his daughter. "Get down here!"

The girl looked up from her explorations, the copper sheen of her hair's cascading curls catching the light of the setting sun. She gave a brief wave before starting down the pyramid's crumbling face, her feet easily and naturally finding secure footing despite the seeming careless rate of her descent. While not so crass as to wish a fall upon her, Carvel resolved that if she did take a tumble she'd have no one to blame but herself.

"Let's take a break," Girnwood said, turning to his young production assistant. "Fifteen minutes, Jerry. We'll shoot the scene, and that should be enough to justify our travel budget to the investors, and we can get the hell out of the jungle and spend the rest of the weekend on holiday in Mérida. Then it's back to Exeter to film the school scenes."

Penny jumped the last few feet to land near her father, a cloud of dust raising from her boots.

"Ladies do not jump, Penelope." Carvel sniffed disapprovingly. It wasn't proper for the young girl be along in the first place. The jungle was, as he understood it, a dangerous place.

"I'm not a lady," Penny said.

"I should say not!"

The little monster stuck out her tongue. "And my name is Penny!"

"Come along, you ragamuffin," her father said. "Apologise to Mr. White."

"I'm sorry, Mr. White." She even sounded sincere, the old actor was impressed.

"As well you should be!" Carvel unbuttoned his jacket — a minor conceit to the heat and humidity. "This wretched jungle is bad enough as is, with its monkeys and highwaymen. The sooner we move on, the better."

"I want to be a monkey. Can I be a monkey, father?"

"You're monkey enough as is, poppet. Let's have no more troubles, dear. The film people need to finish doing their jobs, and then we can leave."

Penny scowled. "Leave? We just got here. I want to explore the pyramid. They're not like the ones in Egypt — you can get inside them and everything!"

"It's a difference in purpose. The ones here were temples, not tombs."

THE TOWER OF BABBAGE

"Do they have magic powers?"

Her father laughed. "What?"

"Kalil said that the pyramids at Giza had magical powers. Because of their shapes. They could make razors sharper and magnets... magnetter!"

"I don't think that's quite true." He glanced back over his shoulder. "It looks like Mr. Girnwood is trapped in the ivy again. Stay away from the front of the pyramid where they're filming."

"Yes, father."

———

Technically Penny was very near the front of the Mayan pyramid, but there were several feet of stone between her and the cameras so she didn't think it counted. She'd never been to the Central American jungles before, and didn't want to waste an opportunity to do a little exploring before they left. She didn't much care for the film people and their movie, particularly the actor-man Mr. White. They were noisy, scaring all the animals away, prone to complaining, and had packed far too much for a simple expedition. Most disappointing was the limited duration of the trip they'd hired her father to guide — a short walk into the rainforest, a few hours at the ruin, then a short hike back to civilisation.

It hardly seemed worth the trouble, but what could one expect? They weren't adventurers like she and father were.

The torch crackled and spat in her hand as she crept through the stone corridors under the ruin. This was more like it. This was the sort of thing she loved most about her life. Most girls her age would be enrolled in some stuffy private day school, or sent to a work house, but she got to travel the world, visiting exotic places, seeing amazing sights. When she grew up she wanted to be just like her father.

No, she'd never heard of a famous girl explorer, but there had to be a first one, right?

Her fingertips traced the ancient carvings set into the walls as she walked along. They didn't look like the ones she'd seen in Egypt, all painted on. These were carved into the stone, square, set in very precise columns.

She stopped, noticing that a section had a slightly different texture, a minor variation in the grain of the carved limestone. While in the same general style as the rest of the designs, there were subtle differences. Penny couldn't really put a name to it, but the figures seemed more... precise. Regular. The limestone was rough, less worn by the passage of millennium.

Penny very nearly gasped as one of the figures, that of a man sitting on a throne, shifted slightly under her fingertips. She touched it again, and found the figure to be on a pivot. The two figures alongside it — a warrior with a spear, and a woman with a jug on her head — proved likewise movable. She listened, ear to the stone, as she turned the central figures. Clicks. Clearly clicks — they formed some kind of stone combination lock.

Her father would have been concerned to have known, but she'd learnt to crack safes from her friend Kalil in Istanbul. There was nothing improper or criminal about it — they were just bored children, hiding in a safe-house while her father dealt with the assassins stalking them — but it passed the time and was a pretty neat trick.

Images of lost Mayan gold filled Penny's head as she turned each of the three figures, an almost inaudible shift in the 'clicks' telling her when she had them in the right position. As the third figure settled into place a section of the wall pivoted inward, exposing a hidden package.

"That's prime," Penny said.

The girl glanced back down the way she'd come. Her father had given her standing orders to come fetch him whenever she'd discovered a secret anything, but for all she knew they were still in the middle of filming — she felt bad enough about interrupting their work earlier, and had no great desire to do so again by popping out of the front entrance unexpectedly. Besides, there was no harm in taking a quick peek, was there?

"I've decided that we're not to have children," Aldora said.

Alton Bartleby, her fiancé, almost dropped his racket mid-serve.

"Fault," his business partner James said without looking up from his work. The engineer was sitting on the lawn alongside the court, jeweller's loupe in his eye, toolkit out, working on his tennis racket with a small screwdriver.

"That's hardly fair," Bartleby said, swinging his own racket aimlessly as he retrieved the ball. "Spouting nonsense to throw me off my game."

"It's not nonsense, it's a simple truth that I've come to understand. We will not be having children."

Aldora was impeccably dressed for lawn tennis in her full-bodied flannel skirt, its hem just above her ankles, matching sailor's hat perched on her head. She constantly rode the edge of fashion in an effortless sort of way, the same way that she navigated the whirls and eddies of London's social rapids with an instinctive grace. The fact that she came from one of the city's great families gave her a considerable advantage, but her ability to navigate it was pure Aldora.

"And I don't suppose I have a say in this?"

Bartleby tossed his ball up again, swinging his racket to the right in a soft slice serve. The ball arced towards the opposite corner of his fiancée's half of the court.

Aldora sidestepped and let the ball bounce before returning it with a forehand swing.

"If Mr. Wainwright can devise a womb for you to carry a child in—"

"No." James said.

In contrast to the expensive leisurewear that his companions wore, the inventor was dressed in utilitarian working-class attire. His cotton trousers were grass-stained, the sleeves of his shirt rolled up to the elbows to spare it from the grease smeared along his hands and forearms.

"There's gossip enough on the length of our engagement as-is," Bartleby said, taking the few steps it took to knock the ball back. "I can only imagine the rumours if we don't produce suitable offspring."

A few brisk steps brought Aldora almost to the net, intercepting the volley. The ball shot to the ground and Bartleby made a lunge, but the bounce carried it well beyond the arc of his swing.

"That was the purpose of this long engagement." Aldora caught the ball as Bartleby threw it to her. "After the marriage we maintain that we're making the attempt for several years. When nothing comes of it, we simply say that we've become too aged to consider it a safe option."

She tossed the ball into the air, then smashed it overhand in a flat serve that skimmed the top of the net. "We'll get some pity for our childless state, but not an undue amount."

"Well." Bartleby returned the serve ably. "We've got Xin Yan. On paper, at least, she's your adoptive daughter."

"On paper," James repeated from the sidelines, snapping his wrist to close the racket he'd been working on.

Not quite a year ago Bartleby and James had been commissioned as consulting detectives to stop a monstrous killer haunting East London. James had discovered young Xin Yan at the site of one of the Scissorman's crime scenes, the sole survivor of the depredations that had taken her family. The engineer didn't take to most people, preferring the solitude of his workroom, but the Chinese girl had grown on him quickly. It wasn't proper that he, a bachelor, be given sole guardianship of a child, so on Bartleby's urging Aldora had taken the girl into her household.

"Let's leave it on paper." Aldora popped the ball back into the air. "Xin Yan is a sweet girl, but the lifestyle I've chosen is not compatible with childcare. Having her as our ward will satisfy our social obligations without the need for our own offspring."

The ball arced, almost skimming the net as it plummeted just on Bartleby's side of the court.

"You will hear no objections from me. Game point."

James took the racket from Bartleby's hand and replaced it with the one he'd been working on.

"What's this?" Bartleby asked.

"It's better."

"Better?" He gave it a practice swing.

"Elastic coils absorb the kinetic energy from the ball's initial impact and release it on the second contact."

"That hardly seems sporting," Bartleby said.

"I've no objection." Aldora tossed the ball up into the air and caught it again. "When you're ready?"

James walked back off the court, while Bartleby once again took up a defencive posture. "Ready."

Aldora lobbed an easy serve towards her fiancé.

Bartleby returned it confidently. "There's a slight hum..."

"It's supposed to do that," James said.

Aldora let the ball bounce, then returned it back towards Alton.

"Here goes—" Bartleby smashed his racket into the ball as it neared him, the strings making an audible twang. The racket's head seemed to blur for just a moment, and the ball shot off like a rocket, narrowly missing Aldora's head and punching a hole in the garden's topiary.

"Well done, Mr. Wainwright," Aldora said, clapping slowly.

"Should it not have done that?"

"No, James," Bartleby said. "It should not have done that."

"What's with the change of heart?" Bartleby asked, escorting Aldora back towards her house. "Regarding offspring, I mean. It wasn't an objection you'd raised before."

"It wasn't a matter we'd discussed before."

"No, but I assumed—"

"Disappointed I shan't be bearing your child, Alton?"

"No," he said. "It's just that we had a plan—"

"Plans change, but the core of our arrangement remains." Aldora glanced up at the sky. "A marriage of convenience that does not interfere with the lifestyles we've chosen."

"We should get around to setting a date, I suppose."

"I fancy a September wedding." Aldora closed her eyes, enjoying the breeze. "That gives us almost a year."

"That suits my needs." Alton pointed towards the house. "You've a visitor."

A carriage had parked in the drive, its coachman waiting idly in his seat.

"I do hope it's not a solicitor," Aldora said, "here on business because

James' racket has lead to a decapitation."

"Be nice."

"I am perfectly civil."

The Fiske's butler met them at the door, posture stiff, shoulders back.

"A messenger awaits you in the hall, Miss," he bowed towards Aldora. "Bearing a certified letter."

"Thank you, Davidson," Aldora handed the man her tennis bonnet. "Inform him that I shall be along presently, after I've had the chance to freshen up."

"Yes, Miss Fiske."

"Go keep the man company, Alton."

"It would be my pleasure," Bartleby grinned. "We'll be in the parlour. Bring us a few drinks, eh, Davidson?"

"Very good, sir."

Aldora joined the men in the waiting parlour, having changed into a light cotton dress with a high-boned collar accenting her neckline, a silk sash around her waist. Alton and her visitor, dressed in full servant's livery, rose as she entered.

"Aldora, darling, I was just talking with Charles here—"

"I am acquainted with Charles," Aldora spoke quietly, an unwelcome lurch in her stomach at the sight of the footman. She spared the pleasantries and stepped to his side. "I was told you had a message. Is it from my parents?"

"Your parents?" Bartleby asked.

"No, Miss Aldora," the ageing footman responded. A gloved hand extended, envelope in hand. "A certified letter arrived for you at your father's home this morning."

Aldora took the envelope with a slight hesitation, eyes scanning the simple scrawling of her name, alone on its back. There was no return address, but the stamp used was international post. "Was this matter brought to my parents' attention?"

"No, Miss," the footman said. "I believed it prudent to avoid burdening them with its arrival."

"Thank you, Charles."

"If I may take my leave—"

"As you would."

The footman bowed once to Bartleby and accompanied the Butler out of the parlour.

Aldora examined the envelope carefully, one finger tracing its edges while Bartleby fidgeted with his hat.

He spoke slowly. "Aldora, your parents—"

"Most of my correspondents possess my current address." Aldora's thoughts were miles away and years in the past. "But those I've not been in contact with recently may mistakenly send missives to my parents' household."

"I see."

"If you would not be terribly insulted, Alton, I am not feeling overly social at the moment."

"Of course, dear," he said, taking his surcoat from the butler. "I will be at the club should you require anything."

"Have a good evening, Alton."

Aldora stood by the parlour window, watching as her fiancé hailed a hansom cab. She stayed there for several minutes, thinking of the man whose signature she'd recognised, before carefully slicing open the top of the envelope with her pen-knife.

"Gentlemen, the call of adventure is upon us."

A chorus of approving harrumphes cascaded through the Gentlemen Explorer's Club's den. While the exclusive club did have a conference room, complete with a long table and chairs, its members were men of Action who did not much stand on the formality of procedure. Instead they stood reading broadsheets or sat with glasses of brandy near the den's cosy fireplace, servants on hand to freshen drinks or snip cigar tips as needed. Many of them, including the club's secretary (currently addressing the collective), were military men.

Colonel Isley had been retired almost a decade, but still dressed in uniform on a day to day basis. He'd returned from India to London several years ago, founding the club with a few other servicemen. It had since expanded to include men of all backgrounds who had a hunger that could only be satiated by adventure, and had managed to fund several such expeditions annually. "What we have before us is a rescue mission to the depths of Mexico's Lacandon Jungles in search of a missing motion picture company."

"Motion picture?" Donaldson, the eldest member of the club leaned forward on his cane, eyes squinted and mouth puckered.

"Cinema. You of course remember the outing in May? We saw the feature on naval shipyards."

"Oh, yes," Donaldson said. "I dare say these cinema men are daft, then, looking for British ships in the jungles of New Spain. No wonder they're in need of rescue."

"They were filming a biographical piece on the life of engineer Charles Babbage. Apparently he'd made a trip to the jungles some five decades ago,

THE TOWER OF BABBAGE

and they deemed it prudent to film along the trail he'd left." Colonel Isley turned to the mirror above the mantle with a snort, smoothing the tips of his imperial moustache. "They were a month overdue for their expected return, and it is feared that they met with a tragic end."

"Is this... Lacandon Jungle... a dangerous place, then?" Donaldson asked the question with a ghoulish grin.

"Dangers abound," the Colonel reported with a smile. "Several species of large cat prowl the area — puma, jaguar, ocelot. And let us not forget the region's volatile politics... Diaz has modernised his nation, but many of his subjects see his policies as needlessly harsh, and the countryside is rife with highwaymen."

"Sounds a right time. Were I a younger man, I would go myself, but these days all my pleasures are vicarious."

The Colonel stirred his drink. "There is a bit of a complication."

"Complication?"

"Our patron, the financier of the proposed expedition, insists upon accompanying us."

"Oh, civilians," Donaldson said. "Money always has its price. As long as he minds us and stays out from underfoot, I've no objection."

"It's a bit more complicated," the Colonel said. "Our patron is one Miss Aldora Fiske."

Silence filled the den, all eyes turning towards the colonel, papers lowered, cigars drooping from hanging jaws.

"And yes. Of those Fiskes."

"A... a woman?" One of the more conservative members folded his broadsheet, placing it on the bar.

"Miss Fiske has repeatedly assured me that she is quite well travelled."

"What does her husband have to say?" Donaldson asked.

"Miss Fiske is engaged to be married to one Alton Bartleby. He has presented no objection."

The silence returned.

"I served with an Alton Bartleby," one of the junior members said. "He was a capable officer."

"Well, if this Bartleby takes responsibility—" the Colonel began.

Donaldson folded his hands. "The Fiskes are a respectable family—"

"If she minds her place—" another member said.

"I feel I should mention that this is perhaps our last opportunity for an expedition this year." The Colonel rolled himself a new cigar. "And we've not the budget to finance anything on our own."

"Let's put a vote to it," a member suggested. "All in favour, say 'Aye?'"

A cascade of members voiced their approval.

"Opposed?"

A scattered handful, Donaldson among them, disagreed.

"Motion is carried. I'll have word sent to Miss Fiske. If you are interested in taking part, report to Mr. Foster so that he knows what measure of provisions to order."

"No good comes of a woman on expedition," Donaldson said. "Bad for morale."

The colonel sipped his tea.

The club treasurer Foster and the military-minded Colonel Isley conducted the expedition's preparations in a brisk and businesslike fashion. Bags of beans and hard-tack, a pound of dried tea-leaves, tents, haversacks, canteens, mosquito netting, malaria pills, extra boots, rifles for the men, and various camp-tools were all gathered. Miss Fiske was content to leave the details to the men, signing bills-of-sale and handing over cheques as required with little question or comment.

Travel was likewise uneventful; a quick freighter across the channel from London to Paris, a train trip to Lisbon, then a pan-Atlantic steam-flight direct to Mérida. In Mexico they'd met with an official who offered moral support for their rescue operation, and warned about peasant uprisings and bandit activity in the area. So warned, the expedition crossed the interior of the Mexican countryside to the jungle. The government had made little attempt to improve the local infrastructure or to exert control beyond taxes, and it wasn't long before the last of the villages on the jungle outskirt was well behind them. The expedition continued afoot, heading in the general direction of the film crew's last known destination: the ancient Mayan ruins of Zipactonal.

"Have you ever been on safari, Miss Fiske?" Colonel Isley asked.

"I've visited the Sundarbans in India—"

"Walking paths formed from the plodding feet of generations of tourists," the Colonel said, leading the way with his machete, hacking away at the thick underbrush. "I am by no means denigrating your holiday experiences, Miss Fiske. Travel is a vital step for citizens of the Empire; we should never forget the larger world that Her Majesty extends dominion over."

"Colonel Isley—"

"But what you must bear in mind regarding these jungles is that they are not so well travelled."

The colonel extended a gloved hand to gently caress the bark of one of the trees.

"They are virginal. Unsullied by the boots of civilised man. Even the locals do not stray far within. The rainforests are the realm of nature, haunted only by bandits and the spirits of the Mayan people, known only by the bones of their ruins."

"I can assure you, Colonel, I am quite aware of our situation." The frost in Aldora's voice was almost enough to wilt the nearby foliage.

He seemed not to notice. "You needn't fret. You travel with military men, and Kelly here a Guild recognised engineer."

"Then I'm sure I feel quite safe." Aldora glanced sidelong at Mr. Kelly, who had been stumbling along beside her. "Though I am surprised to see an Engineer so willing to leave his laboratory to go striding about the jungle, Mr.Kelly."

Like the others Kelly had dressed for the expedition in rugged khaki with belted bush jackets, and a pith helmet. Unlike Colonel Isley, however, Kelly did not wear his outfit with ease. The jacket hung loose off his frame, and he seemed to be having considerable difficulty keeping his helmet steady on his head. In Aldora's estimation this was the first time he'd ever been on a wilderness excursion.

"I will admit that this is not the environment I am accustomed to," Kelly said, looking up at the thick canopy overhead. "I am not personally one for fieldwork, but this was an opportunity I could not let pass me by."

"Do go on." Aldora herself was not so gauche as to wear trousers, even so far from London's watching eyes and wagging tongues, but she had sacrificed her haute couture skirts for athletic bloomers fastened just below the knees. She had shouldered her knapsack without complaint, politely declining the Colonel's repeated offers to carry it for her.

The engineer's cultured nasal voice seemed to fill the air as the party continued, adopting that lecturing cadence that Aldora frequently pretended not to be bothered by. "In many ways my career has been following in Babbage's footsteps. I first studied and then emulated his work during my Guild apprenticeship, and then chose analytical engines as my speciality as I embarked as a journeyman."

"Analytical engine?" Colonel Isley paused to take a quick drink from his canteen. "I'm afraid that I'm only familiar with combat engineering."

"At the Academy there was a saying — 'to the flash goes the funding.' Kelly flashed a painful smile. "It's easier to explain airship engines and lightning cannons to the public, but it'll be analytical engines that change the world. Imagine it — mechanical devices capable of thousands of arithmetic calculations an hour, logical control flow with conditional branches and loops... integrated memory..."

The Colonel narrowed his eyes slightly. "Yes, it all sounds very complicated, but what do they do?"

"Thinking machines," Kelly said. "They'll let one Engineer do the work of hundreds. Innovation and design will progress at a rate that will make the last hundred years' rushed advancement look like a snail's pace."

"That sounds dreadful and short-sighted." The Colonel shook his head, stooping to examine a patch of mud.

"Short-sighted?" Aldora asked.

"Work too fast and they'll run out of things to invent." The Colonel stood, gaze panning from side to side, speaking with some distraction. "Then they'll have to get real jobs."

"With all due respect, Colonel—" Kelly began, stumbling over his words.

"Someone passed by, not too long ago."

"Bandits?" Kelly asked, moving closer.

"Boots." The Colonel waved the engineer away. "Natives would go barefoot or sandalled, I should think, and the tread on these prints is too sturdy for simple highwaymen, unless purloined. I would presume military."

"That does not bode well," Aldora said.

"Let us men worry about such unpleasantries," Isley said. "We'll keep you safe, have no fear."

After a few moments the Colonel started walking again. "They're at least an hour ahead of us. Continue your story, Kelly."

"Yes, well. That Babbage travelled to Mexico is well known, but what he aimed remains a great mystery. He told no one of his intentions, swore the workmen who accompanied him to secrecy, and burned all records of his journey upon his return."

"Quite the mystery," Aldora said.

"It most likely has something to do with the Mayan ruins he was visiting, though what, none can say for sure."

"Weren't the Mayans known for their own clockwork astronomical relics?" Isley asked.

"All we have to go on is the writing of the Spanish conquistadors," Kelly said. "They left little of what they encountered intact. All that remains in the ruins are what wasn't valuable and would not burn."

"Pity, that," Aldora said. "The boots of military men tromping once more across the face of history."

"I can assure you, Miss Fiske," Colonel Isley said, puffing his chest out. "The Royal Military takes the greatest of care when dealing with an indigenous people's cultural heritage."

"I meant to imply nothing to the contrary," Aldora said, thinking the man looked quite the quail.

The Colonel harrumphed.

THE TOWER OF BABBAGE

As the sun set Isley called for a stop along a winding stream. He worked quickly but diligently to set up the camp despite Kelly's help, while Aldora erected her own shelter a short ways away.

"I'm afraid you may find travel fare a bit lacking compared to what your household staff prepares, Miss Fiske," Colonel Isley said, watching as Mr. Kelley built a fire.

"As I have mentioned multiple times, I am well familiar with wilderness travel." She had resolved to patiently repeat it until it managed to penetrate the thickness of the Colonel's skull.

"Yes, well. I am sure that you will find that Lacandon a tad more 'wilderness' than the sunny coasts of Brighton."

"Colonel Isley," Aldora wheeled on the man, tent stake in hand.

"I can assure you that I am an experienced world traveller. In addition to the jungles of India, I have ridden wild stallions in the American west, snowshoed the wilds of northern Canada, sailed the Barbary Coast, and toured the Arabian desert." Her patience exhausted, each named destination was punctuated with a step forward, and the Colonel found himself forced back by the ire in the woman's gaze. "Am I clear?"

"Yes." The Colonel managed, pushing the tip of Aldora's tent stake aside. "Quite."

"Good." Aldora turned and returned to her tent, hammering in the last of the stakes.

Kelly watched her with some surprise. "That's... more travel than I would gather most woman of your calibre are familiar with."

A flush came to Aldora's neck and face. "Forgive me... I mention it not out of braggadocio, but to save the Colonel the bother of having to explain and condescend to me the basics of travel beyond the Empire's borders."

He chuckled, then lowered his voice. "You needn't justify yourself to me, Miss. Frankly, I was almost as tired of the old man's blather as you. I'm only surprised you bore as much of it as you did."

Aldora gave a relieved chuckle. "While Colonel Isley may be an exceptional chauvinist, I am sorry to say that the vaunted halls of London society are no strangers to the perils of misogyny."

"You— ah, you're engaged to Mr. Alton Bartleby?"

"Oh yes," Aldora said. "The dear. I do so hope he is getting on well without me."

"Ah. I was engineer on the Benbow while he served there. Good man, from what I'd heard."

Aldora froze a moment, then turned towards the man slowly. "Mr.

Kelly."

"Yes?"

"My fiancé does not much advertise his naval service..."

"I don't see why not. He was a capable lieutenant, and well regarded by the men—"

"His reasons are his own, but he has taken pains to counter rumours of his military past within the city of London. We would both be appreciative if you did not undo his careful work."

Kelley nodded. "I don't quite understand, but I'll respect his privacy."

"Thank you, Mr. Kelley."

It was a small sound that woke Aldora from her slumber, a tiny noise easily overlooked in a strange place after a long day's march. Many would have written it off as the normal sounds of jungle life, or as one of her companions shifting in their tents, but there was a quality to it that roused the gentlewoman immediately and had her reaching for the pistol she habitually kept under her pillow.

It was the sound of exaggerated care, and she had long ago learnt the difference between the courtesy of quiet and the treachery of stealth.

Aldora was as quiet as the campsite's stalker had intended to be, rolling to the back of her tent and quickly slipping into her boots while her ears strained to hear the absence of noise. There were several of them, a group, moving into position to descend upon the camp in unison. Before she was even awake enough to process this and what it might mean the pen-knife was in her hand, cutting a slit through the back of her tent. She slipped through it soundlessly, cringing slightly at the noise she'd made brushing against the fabric, fancying that all ears were attuned to her every motion.

It might have been that small sound that set off the attack, or it may have simply been time, but no sooner had she ducked into the foliage than did come shouts and gunfire behind her.

"*Se toma a la mujer,*" a rough voice called. "*Voy a por el viejo loco!*"

"*Enrique se ha desaparecido!*" came an answering cry.

She plunged headlong through the underbrush, sharp jungle leaves and thorns tearing at her hands and sleeping gown, dampness making its thin cotton cling to her body, threatening to tangle up about her legs.

She couldn't hear pursuit following over the noise she was making stumbling through the bushes and ferns between the trees, but instinct drove her on, certain her that dangerous men with rifles were but steps behind her.

Aldora pushed clear from the bushes into empty space, uncontrolled

THE TOWER OF BABBAGE

momentum carrying her out over a steep ravine.

Gravity grabbed her, smashing her against the muddy slope.

She tucked the best she could as she tumbled down, bowling over small thorny brush and saplings before plunging into the cool depths of a river's waters.

Aldora thrashed for a moment towards the surface before a sudden fear of beasts hidden in the dark water struck her spine. Such creatures were attracted to the jerky motion, sure signs of wounded prey, and she adjusted to push against the water with long smooth strokes.

After righting herself in the water and rediscovering equilibrium she swam with the current towards what she believed to be the closer bank.

Fingers torn by jungle bushes and numbed by the cold water scrabbled at the shore. Weighed down by her sodden nightclothes, Aldora managed to pull herself from the current and onto the shore, where she lay panting and gasping for breath.

"*Antal-ot ma'alob?*" came a voice in the darkness, speaking a language that she didn't recognise. "*Mina'an aanta?*"

Aldora's eyes searched the blackness, but could not see the speaker. He was near, though, next to her.

"Okay," she managed, closing her eyes, beaten and exhausted. "I give up. I surrender. *Me rindo.*"

Strong hands grasped her, picked her up, but she was too disoriented and battered to struggle. It was best, she maintained, to endure the indignities an enemy might visit upon one when defenceless, and then attack from a point of power later. Spaniards were — if anything — even more chauvinistic than her own countrymen, and the bandits of Mexico were probably no different. She was, to them, only a woman, and for now that was her greatest asset. It was an all-too common weakness in others that she was quite happy to exploit.

To her surprise her captor did not take her back across the river to the camp to rendezvous with the others, but instead trod swiftly through the jungle, hoisting Aldora over his shoulder. She was surprised to see that he wore his hair long, almost to the small of his back, and he was dressed in a simple cloth tunic. She allowed herself the small hope that he wasn't one of the bandits that had raided her camp.

Aldora found herself carried to a small village of primitive palm-thatched huts.

"*Le'!*" the native carrying her shouted. "*Inkaxan ixoq ka mina'an aanta!*"

A number of figures appeared in the hut entrances, dressed in cotton tunics, men and women both with long hair. They stared through the darkness at Aldora, an old man bringing a lit torch closer as he peered at her face.

"*Tu'ux kaxan?*" the elder native asked.

The other native put her down, helping her stand steady. "*Tumen ja'l. Leti' púuts'ul máak.*"

"Please," Aldora made the appeal to those around her, her eyes flashing from face to face. "Do any of you speak English? *Alguno de ustedes habla Español?*"

The natives returned blank stares, muttering to one another in hushed tones.

"*Taas tzeb?*" the one who had brought her asked.

"*Wáa,*" the elder replied. He turned towards Aldora, speaking in a slow sing-song and extending his hand. "*Bin tutséel... bin, bin.*"

Aldora let herself be lead by the old native towards a central hut lit by glowing embers. The elder ducked within, then gestured that she should follow. "*Bin, bin.*"

Inside waited a young girl, lighter of feature than the others, though her tunic was of the same simple cotton, and her matted hair was just as long. She stared at Aldora's dishevelled state, her muddy hair, her scratched skin, her torn nightgown.

"Hello?" Aldora said, feeling acutely self-conscious in a way that she hadn't with the other natives moments before.

"You — you're English?" the girl stammered.

"Yes." Aldora said, a flood of relief washing through her. "Yes, I am."

"Are you here to rescue me?" the girls eyes cast across Aldora's ruined nightgown.

"I... my party had come to the jungle in search of a missing film crew."

"That's me!" The girl scrambled to her feet. "I mean, I was a part of that expedition, with my father."

"I'm afraid I'm not in much shape to rescue anyone at the moment," Aldora said, putting a hand on the girl's shoulder to steady her. "Highwaymen ambushed our camp. I alone managed to escape."

The girl's face fell and she seemed almost to collapse in on herself. "Oh... that's what happened to me. They took everyone, but I escaped."

Aldora studied the disheartened girl silently for a long moment. It was obvious that she was trying her best not to cry. She half-raised a hand to comfort her, but let it fall to her side, not sure exactly what to say or do. Helplessness wasn't something she was well acquainted with.

"Some rescue we turned out to be. My name is Aldora."

"I'm Penny," the girl responded.

"How long have you been here, with these people?"

THE TOWER OF BABBAGE

"The *Hach Winik*?" Penny asked. "I don't know. What month is this?"

Penny's story was brief. She'd emerged from some ruin exploration to find the film crew face to face with a force of bandits. Her appearance had galvanised the armed men into action, and much confusion had ensued as they were taken prisoner. She'd slipped away, escaping into the jungle, where she wandered for several days before the natives had found her and taken her in. They'd given her months of hospitality, during which she'd learnt their language and some of their ways.

"You managed to survive the jungle on your own for days?" Aldora asked. "That's... impressive."

"I've been travelling with my father since I was a little girl. I know all the tricks." Her smile faltered and then faded. "I do hope he's alright."

One of the Hach Winik women arrived with bowls of a thick broth. She smiled and handed one to each of the women, then backed out of the hut.

"Eat it, it's good," Penny said. "But very spicy."

"Oh, yes," Aldora held the bowl from her face. "I should say so."

Penny grinned, then made a show of taking a large gulp from the edge of the bowl.

"Your father — was he one of the crew?" Aldora asked.

"Their guide. Henry Robinson."

"Henry?" Aldora's hand tightened around the rim of the bowl. "You're Henry's daughter, then."

Penny took a smaller sip. "Did you know my father?"

"Yes, a long time ago. He... ah." She took a small sip. "He had a letter set to be delivered to me if he didn't return to Mérida, giving me the details of the expedition. That's why I've come."

"Ohhh." Penny nodded. "As long as I can remember he'd been leaving letters behind whenever we went on expedition. I never knew who they were addressed to, only that they were someone he trusted."

"It's an old traveller's trick," Aldora said. "I've left one behind to be delivered to my fiancé."

"Aren't you a little old to be engaged?" Penny asked.

"How old do you think I am, young lady?"

"I dunno," Penny said. "Forty?"

"I am twenty-nine years of age, not that it's any of your business, and it has been a long engagement."

Penny sipped her broth. "No need to be cross with me, Miss. I'm never getting married."

"Never?" Aldora's frost melted a little as she reminded herself of what the girl had been through.

"Not ever. I'm just going to travel forever, like my father, and never settle down in any one place."

Aldora smiled wanly. "I'd wanted much the same when I was not much older than you. Unfortunately the realities of my own family prohibited it."

"I've never understood why adults don't simply do whatever it is that they want."

"You will when you're older."

"That's what father says... but he doesn't follow any rules but his own."

"Sometimes one's own laws can be harsher than any others. Particularly for a man like your father."

Penny didn't respond. The native woman returned, this time with a pile of quilted blankets that she deposited next to Aldora.

"How long do you think it'll take for your letter to get to your fiancé?"

"I gave myself weeks to find your party," Aldora said, spreading the thickest quilt along the hut's dirt floor. "It's a big jungle. Give it another week or so to reach Alton, give him a week to arrange a rescue..."

"That's not so long."

"Even so, I've no intention of waiting around for another rescue party." Aldora settled in to the nest of quilts she'd assembled, leaving her dressing-gown to dry above the embers. "Every day that passes makes finding your father and the crew less likely."

"What else can we do? Leave the jungle ourselves and get help?"

"We shall see, Penny." Aldora closed her eyes. "We'll see how things look by dawn's light."

The next morning brought a hearty and lightly spiced meal of cornmeal flatbread and beans, and the natives brought Aldora a simple white cotton tunic, identical to the ones they themselves wore. It was plain, unadorned and shaped only by the curves of her body, but fell to an acceptably modest length, almost to the ground. Her nightgown, torn to shreds, was given as a gift to the woman serving as their host. She seemed grateful for the silk.

The Hach Winik hunter who had brought her to the village returned as Aldora and Penny were finishing up their breakfast. By the light of day he was quite handsome in a healthy and exotic way, with bronze skin, strong facial features, and an athletic physique. His long hair hung freely, cascading around his broad shoulders.

"Amoxtli says that he went back to your campsite," Penny translated, "But all of your things were missing."

"Bloody highwaymen," Aldora said. "Forgive my language."

"I don't think that they were bandits, though. They had uniforms and acted like soldiers."

"Mexican army?"

THE TOWER OF BABBAGE

"I don't think so. They seemed like mercenaries."

Aldora finished lacing up her boots. "Oh? And what does a young girl know of mercenaries?"

Penny frowned. "Father's business had us associating with all sorts of people."

"Terribly irresponsible of Henry. It's hardly proper for a young girl to know the company of such men."

The girl stuck out her tongue. "It's no less proper for a lady of your rarefied station."

Aldora's face coloured, a bitter retort on her lips until she remembered what the girl had been through. Her harsh look softened, and she shook her head. "Regardless of who they are they have taken your father and the others. What do you know of them?"

"The Hach Winik call them the Strangers," Penny said. "They've been gathering in the jungle for some time, but after they ran across us at the ruins of Zipactonal they moved their camp there. Amoxtli says that they spend all day going into and out of the temple."

"Do they hold captives?"

Penny nodded. "He's not sure how many though."

"Can... Amoxtli... get us to a place where we can observe the camp safely?"

"I'll ask," Penny said. "Why? Do you have a plan?"

"Waiting for another rescue attempt is not an option — now the mercenaries will surely realise that more searchers will be coming, and move their camp, possibly deeper into the jungle. We must act ourselves. We have to rescue your father and the others before they... before they move on."

Penny nodded, biting her lip, then translated Aldora's question to the tribesman.

Aldora lowered her eyes, unable to face the girl directly. Things were more dire than she could let on. Mercenaries were not known for keeping superfluous prisoners. Carvel White, the actor, could be ransomed, and the director came from a family with money, but the others — the crew, the military men from the club, and poor, poor sweet Henry... she couldn't fret. Not now, not in front of the girl. The highwaymen had taken everything she'd brought, and all that she and Penny had left was hope. She couldn't take that hope away.

"Amoxtli says he can take us," Penny said, excitement in his voice.

"Good man," Aldora flashed the man a brief smile. "Off with us, then."

"What do you see?" Penny asked.

"It's an encampment." Aldora, Penny, and Amoxtli lay on a ridge some distance away from the ruins, where dozens of tents had been set up in a semi-circle around the temple itself. She counted six sentries, placed at strategic points radiating out from the temple, but the camp provided for many more. Most alarming, perhaps, were the pair of artillery cannons flanking the ruins' entrance, pointed towards the trail heading back into the jungle. "They look dug-in and prepared. There are amenities for dozens of soldiers, but I don't see more than a handful."

"Amoxtli said that they spend most of their time inside the ruins."

"What's in there?"

"Just before... before the men arrived I was exploring the temple, and I found a secret passage. It was dark inside — too dark for me to see, but it was massive space. "

"Fascinating," Aldora said. "Any indication of what was inside?"

Penny gave the matter some thought. "I think I felt what might have been some clockworks? I can't be sure. Oh, and I could hear running water."

"Clockworks and running water? Are you positive?"

"I told you it was dark. There was something in there, though."

"No matter. It was rather brave of you to go exploring in the dark on your own."

Penny grinned. "That's just the life father and I live, Miss Fiske. Exploring ancient ruins, running from bandits, crossing wild jungles..."

She trailed off, her smile being replaced by worry.

"Amoxtli..." Aldora said.

The native turned his head, giving Aldora a winning smile.

"Penny, would you ask Amoxtli if he knows of any caves or subterranean rivers in the area?"

"Subterranean rivers?"

"That water you heard had to come from somewhere. We might not be able to easily sneak through the camp to the ruins—"

"But if there's another way in, we can come up under them and rescue the captives!"

Aldora nodded, pleased with the girl's enthusiasm.

Penny translated Aldora's question to the native. He responded at length, pointing off into the distance several times.

"Amoxtli says that there is an old story of the ancestors. When the Strangers first came in the time of his grandfather's fathers, the people retreated to the temple for safety. The women and children escaped through tunnels into the jungle, where they hid. He says that one of these tunnels comes out in a nearby cave."

"He may be speaking of the conquistadors," Aldora said. "The Hack Wilek must be descendant from the ancient Mayan people. They escaped and hid in the jungles, where they've gone unnoticed living their old ways for centuries."

Aldora backed away from the edge, then rose to her feet. "It just may be what we need to save the captives."

"*Pa'tal, ko'olel,*" Amoxtli said, voice low. "*Yan peets' hach k'as aktun! Yan ts'aakik yan e'hoch'e'en.*"

"He says that when his people escaped, they left traps behind to deter pursuit," Penny said. "It may be dangerous."

"Does he know where they are?"

Penny turned her head towards the native. "*Na'atik tu'ux peets'?*"

He shook his head. "*Chowak ora. Biyeho k'iin maak.*"

"Only vague stories remain."

"We'll have to risk it," Aldora said. "I see no other way to retrieve the captives. Return to the village, Penelope — we'll return for you once I've secured your father."

"I'll do nothing of the sort." Penny folded her arms. "I've been in the ruins, and you haven't. And you may still need me to translate for Amoxtli!"

"Child, it's far too dangerous for me to even consider..."

"I've been running from thugs and evading traps in ancient ruins since I was eight. And... and it's my father, Miss Fiske. I can't — I cannot just wait for you to save him."

Aldora's face softened at the tears in the girl's eyes. "If I allow you to accompany us, you must do precisely what I say, when I say it."

"I understand, Miss."

"Very well then."

Aldora spared a last glance at the camp below. Ordinarily she would not even consider letting the girl tag along, but there was just something about Penelope that reminded Aldora of herself as a child. If they were as alike as she believed they were, an order to return to the camp would have simply lead the girl to tagging along at a distance, putting herself in even greater danger, and leading to potential exposure for all of them. It was safer to keep the wilful girl at her side.

The cavern entrance sat a short distance away, half-way up a short bluff, its mouth obscured with hanging vines. The tribesman cleared them away with the butt of his spear, then gestured towards the darkness beyond. He cast about briefly, gathered a bundle of rushes from under the bluff's overhang, and fashioned them into a crude torch. After lighting it with a primitive fire-drill, he stepped into the cavern entrance, followed by the girls.

Aldora was impressed with the way the people of the Lacandon managed to get by without modern technology, using the natural resources of the wilderness to meet their needs. It was so different from what the Empire had become, dependent on its engineering, dependent on the innovations of its Guild of Artificers to compete with the powerhouses of America and Prussia. The closest to self-sufficiency Britain got were the lowest classes, forced to adapt the available urban resources to their needs. Those of her own social class would be helpless without the infrastructure they'd built on the backs of the working class.

The Empire's growing dependency had never sat well with her. Unlike her fiancé who cheerfully exploited the system for what it was worth, Aldora despised being beholden to anyone.

The cave's walls were naturally smooth, carved with various blocky symbols, both abstract and geometric. Each block was part of a column, and the columns were paired off at regular intervals.

"What does it say?"

"Ba'ax xook?" Penny asked.

"Xookik ma' ts'iib," Amoxtli held the torch up to examine the carvings. *"Mixbik'in na'atik. K'aax, ma' papah."*

"He says he doesn't know — he's a hunter, not a priest." Penny glanced back towards the entrance. "There's a priest in the village. Should we get him?"

"The old man?" Aldora asked. "It's not worth exposing him to danger, and I'd rather not let the captives wait much longer. Every moment counts. Let's go on."

Amoxtli's torch flickered and spattered as they moved through the cave, irregularities in the walls creating patterned shadows among the hieroglyphs. Blind cave beetles and lizards scampered away from the vibrations of their footfalls, retreating to just inside the radius of their light, like a constantly receding tide.

After a few hundred feet the tunnel merged with a cross running underground stream. It looked as though the water had, long ago, crashed through a stone wall, above which was carved another Mayan glyph.

"Amoxtli says that that's Huracan, another storm god... this one was responsible for flooding the earth at the end of the last cycle."

"Interesting parallel to the biblical food," Aldora said. "And possibly a trap, one long triggered by the Spaniards pursuing his fleeing ancestors."

"Is there a way around?"

"I don't think so," Aldora said. "I think the trap was the sudden rush of water. The current seems swift, but not unmanageable, and it isn't terribly deep. We can just forge through."

Penny translated for the tribesman, and he nodded, pulling the cotton tunic off over his head. Instinctively Aldora looked away, doing her best not to steal a glance at Amoxtli bronze flesh, his long, lean muscles, his unabashed nudity.

"The Lacandon don't have much modesty," Penny said.

Aldora stared into the water, definitely not noticing the way that the man's abdominal muscles stretched as he wrapped the tunic around the crown of his head. She cleared her throat. "Still, it would hardly be proper for us to be so exposed before a strange man."

"What if he went ahead of us?" Penny asked.

"Yes, that would do quite nicely," Aldora answered quickly.

Penny translated, and Amoxtli gave a noncommittal shrug before taking the lead, wading into the water without a care, its depth coming up to the small of his back. Aldora followed after him, holding her tunic above her head, acutely aware of the water caressing her hips and the bottom of her ribs, her breasts exposed to the cool air, while Penny brought up the rear, submerged to her shoulders. The current's incessant urging brought them along swiftly.

Their lead stopped and half-turned towards Aldora, who quickly covered her chest with her folded tunic. A grin quirked at the corner of his mouth, and he pointed at an engraved glyph in the ceiling. "*Cabrakan — lu'um yat Xibalba. Yat ha' taam.*"

"Cabrakan," Penny translated. "God of earthquakes. He also says that there's a drop off in the water ahead."

"Another trap," Aldora said, wading forward. "Triggered prior to the water trap. Perhaps a collapsing floor?"

"It's amazing that the Ancestors had the time to build these traps while running from the Spaniards."

Amoxtli had secured his tunic on his head and began to swim forward, torch held aloft. Aldora followed his example, wrapping her own tunic around her hair. "It's more reasonable to assume that they built this escape tunnel long before the conquistadors arrived. For protection against whom, though, I cannot say."

The group swam along until coming to a climbable bank. Aldora covered Penny's eyes while Amoxtli emerged and donned his tunic. The girls, after making sure that he wasn't watching, followed after, using the sturdy roots that emerged from the earthen bank to pull themselves up before dressing.

A broad but still limestone pool spanned the width of the tunnel ahead; Amoxtli examined it critically while waiting for the girls to catch their breath.

He glanced up towards the ceiling, pointing towards an engraving of a hook-nosed man in a headdress. "*Chaak. U peek chaak. Ch'iin baat.*"

"He says that that's Chaak. One of their gods. He's a god of rain and storms and lightning."

Aldora nodded. "Lightning. Hm. Hold on a second."

She stepped to the tunnel wall, clearing the vines away from a section to reveal black and richer green veins in the pale limestone. "See those striations in the limestone? I think that they're copper."

"Copper?"

"Not just copper. Iron as well. They run the length of the walls to that carving, and down into a ring formation below. This may be another one of the traps the ancient Mayans constructed."

"I don't see how."

She turned to Amoxtli and gestured towards his spear. "May I?"

He grunted, handing it over.

Aldora put the tip to the floor and brought her foot down sharply just below its flint head, snapping it off cleanly.

"Pa'tal!" he protested.

Aldora picked up the spear's head, cleaned it off, took aim, and then skipped it across the surface of the pool. Small trails of sparks kicked up from the water wherever it landed.

"What?" Penny stared in awe.

"Copper and iron are never found in limestone," Aldora explained, handing the spear's shaft back to the tribesman. "They had to have been placed there with intent, and if that god Chaak is a lightning god... copper, iron, and an electrolyte like saltwater are all it takes to make a simple battery."

"I had no idea that the Mayans were capable of making things like that," Penny said.

"Nor I, but from what I've read they left behind a legacy of mysterious clockworks that the Europeans of the time could scarcely comprehend. Primitive batteries — even on such a scale as this — do not seem beyond their capabilities."

"How do we get across?"

Aldora examined the walls and ceilings. "There are creeper vines holding fast to the cavern. If we are brave enough to chance it, we can attempt a climb, though I'll warn you that it shan't be easy."

THE TOWER OF BABBAGE

She looked back from the wall to where Penny had been, only to find the girl gone. Aldora glanced around in alarm, finally spotting the girl clambering up the wall to the ceiling as nimble as a capuchin, fingers grabbing handfuls of vine.

"Penny wait! We don't know if the roots will support us!"

"Seems strong enough to me."

Having reached the ceiling, Penny hung by her fingers, crossing easily, hand over hand, all the way across the deadly expanse of electric-charged water.

Aldora watched in awe and horror, waiting for the fall that never occurred.

Penny dropped to the ground on the other side. "Made it!"

"You've scared me nearly to death." Aldora managed.

She crossed to the other tunnel wall, examined the vines, and removed her sandals, and almost delicately began to climb.

Unlike Penny she didn't care to test the ceiling's vines' tensile strength, instead using the lattice of vegetation to climb sideways across the wall above the pool.

She dismounted upon reaching the other side, and glanced across the water to where Amoxtli was taking a few steps back away from the water, broken spear shaft held in his hands.

"I don't know if the roots would support Amoxtli weight," Aldora said. "Perhaps you should tell him to go back and wait—"

With a long cry the Lacandon tribesman ran forward, leaping as he reached the edge of the pool, leaping through the air like a jaguar.

He tucked and rolled as he landed, clearing the water, and coming to his feet next to the girls.

Penny clapped her hands. "Prime jump! That had to be at least six yards!"

"Yes," Aldora said, gazing at the guide's long muscular legs with a new appreciation. "Quite impressive."

Amoxtli gave a smile that brought a small blush to the gentlewoman's cheeks. "Ma' Bartel."

Penny laughed. "Hooch suit'!"

Aldora forced her eyes away from the lines of the Lacandon man's form. "Let's continue."

"There's a ladder here," Penny put a hand on one of its rungs, carved into the stone wall. "It's lit up above."

"Amoxtli will go first," Aldora said. "And then I. You come up when I tell you it's safe."

Penny nodded, stepping back, and allowing the Lacandon to make his way up the stairs.

"You fancy him don't you." Penny whispered.

She couldn't tell that Aldora's face had reddened in the darkness as their guide's torch had ascended with him. "That is not an acceptable topic of conversation."

"Yeah, but you do, don't you. A right buck, he is. Want me to crack you up to him?"

"That's enough cheek out of you, young lady." Aldora mounted the ladder, following up after Amoxtli.

She emerged into a tunnel lit with a gas lantern hanging on a hook. It wasn't until she turned to look behind her that she noticed the harsh uniformed men with rifles holding the guide silent. It took all of her willpower to avoid glancing down the ladder towards Penny as she audibly gasped, raised her hands, and backed away, just managing to hope that the girl would take the hint and stay hidden below.

The mercenaries remained silent as they escorted Aldora and Amoxtli through lamp-lit tunnels, and Aldora didn't volunteer any information herself. The uniforms they wore reminded her of those used by the Spanish infantry, but they were more subdued, a grey rather than light blue, rank insignia on the shoulders rather than the cuffs. Their hats were straw, in the style of the Mexican charro's Sombrero. The uniforms had not withstood the jungle's rigour with grace, but the men's rifles seemed in excellent condition.

While the uniforms were nationalistically identifiable, Aldora noted that the men themselves were not. Of the three escorting them, two looked Hispanic, and the third possibly Eastern European. Russian, perhaps.

The tunnel opened up into a massive chamber filled with levels of wooden scaffolding built around a towering cubic clockwork structure. Its purpose wasn't immediately apparent, shifting gears arranged around sliding flywheels, pneumatic tubes snaking between steam-powered pistons, hinged flanges tapping staccato rhythms that echoed throughout the structure. Beyond the guards walking slowly along the scaffolding she could see a man in ragged safari-wear examining the mechanism — Mr. Kelley?

Set around the tower and its base were caches of supplies: barrels of food and water, bundles of cloth, kegs of cordite and shot for the cannons outside.

One of the mercenaries prodded her along with the barrel of his rifle, preventing her from taking in any more detail, and the prisoners were escorted down a side tunnel. A vine-tied wooden lattice had been placed across its far end, and two of the mercenaries stood watch as the third moved it aside.

Aldora and Amoxtli were prodded through into a small cell where two men — one in a ruined tweed waistcoat and trousers, the other in torn safari khakis — sat along its walls.

"Miss Fiske!" Colonel Isley scrambled to his feet. His face was dirt smudged, and his impeccable moustache looked ragged."Thank heavens you're alive!"

And now they know my name, Aldora cursed inwardly. Thank you for that.

"Are you alright? We'd feared the worst."

Aldora hesitated, waiting until the guards' echoing footsteps had faded. "After the raid I was taken in by the local native people."

"You're the woman who financed this rescue operation?" Aldora recognised the other man as the actor Carvel White. "I cannot say that I am impressed."

"You know how it is. Things seldom work out as intended."

"What the devil are you wearing?"

"It's a tunic the natives were kind enough to lend me."

"It's dreadful."

The Colonel frowned. "You'd rather she traipse around in her all-together?"

Carvel gave Aldora an appraising look. "I should say not. I prefer my women with a more classical figure."

"I shall endeavour to recover from such stunning disappointment. If you are quite through critiquing my apparel, where are the others?"

"Dead, I am sad, but not surprised to say," Carvel said. "Our production assistant was killed in the initial assault. Our guide slain as an example when he refused to show the mercenaries' commander whatever respect the bastard felt entitled to."

Hank Robinson is dead. Aldora sat down heavily, hand flitting to her face. It took a lot to take the wind out of Aldora's sails, to wreck her poise, to slip the mask of perfect composure from her face. Carvel didn't seem to notice.

"I haven't seen Mr. Girnwood, the director, since our capture, but I assume that he's dead as well."

"No," Aldora spoke absently, distracted. "He comes from a wealthy family. He'll be kept separate from the rest of us for ransom."

"That cannot be," Carvel said. "I'm a universally well-regarded symbol of the stage. If anyone's worth a ransom, I am."

"Perhaps he's not a fan of theatre," Isley suggested. "Mr. Kelley was taken as well."

"I think I might have spotted him," Aldora said. "Working on that giant clockwork."

"What do you suppose its purpose might be?"

"I haven't the foggiest." Aldora looked over at Carvel. "How did Mr. Robinson die?"

"Foolishly," Carvel said with a snort. "The director, Mr. Girnwood, was trying to wheedle some sort of deal with the mercenary commander, throwing his weight and reputation around, and quite simply exhausted the man's patience. He struck the man, and Robinson called him out as a coward for assaulting a bound prisoner. He was shot as an example to the rest of us."

"An example."

"So he said. It seemed to have been an effective one, at least for Girnwood."

Aldora forced herself to focus. "And what sort of man is this mercenary commander?"

"You'll find out yourself," a gruff voice from behind her spoke. A new pair of guards had silently appeared at the door, rifles at ready. "Come with us, Miss. *Y tu tambien, hombre.*"

The latter was directed at Amoxtli. Aldora rose, interposing herself between the men and her guide. "You don't need him. He's a native — he doesn't speak English or Spanish."

"That's up to the commander. Come along."

The guards escorted Aldora and Amoxtli past the clockwork tower and through darkened corridors to the dusk outside beyond the temple's entrance, and to a large central pavilion tent. It was dark and sombre within, lit by beeswax candles, decorated with Catholic iconography. A portable altar had been set up at the far end, flanked by tall standards bearing a severe and geometric Christian styling. The fore of the tent was occupied with rows of folding chairs of wood and cloth.

The man occupying the tent was dressed in a uniform similar to the other mercenaries, over which he wore a black Catholic clerical waistcoat, buttoned all the way up to the collar. To Aldora his ensemble gave the impression of a militant cassock, made all the more blatant by the gun-belt slung along his hips. He was tall, dark, and athletic, with a regal Hispanic bearing that well suited the pavilion tent's atmosphere.

The guards stopped just outside to flank the tent's entrance.

"Miss Fiske, I presume?" The militant priest looked up as she and Amoxtli entered.

Aldora placed his accent as educated Barcelonian. "I am afraid you have the advantage."

His smile did not reach his eyes. "Father Jago Sarsosa. I apologise for the circumstances."

"Charmed. Should I call you Father Sarsosa or Commander Sarsosa?"

"You may refer to me as is your pleasure, Miss Fiske."

She grinned unpleasantly. "Be careful with your permissions, Commander, I may just take you up on them."

Sarsosa's smile didn't falter. Everything about the man, Aldora noted, was impeccable. His pocket kerchief was folded just so. His moustache was waxed to the perfect degree. His hair parted expertly down the middle.

This was a man who prided himself on his control, perhaps to a pathological degree.

He addressed Amoxtli. "And you, sir?"

Aldora spoke quickly. "He is only a simple native guide. Speaks nothing but his tribal tongue."

Sarsosa studied the man carefully before apparently dismissing him as unimportant. "Very well. Let us not unduly waste one another's' time, Miss Fiske. You financed the expedition to find your filmmakers, so it is obvious that you come from money. Are you married?"

"Why, Father Sarsosa. That's rather forward of you."

"Miss Fiske."

"I am engaged to be married."

"Then it is to your father that I should address your ransom."

"You would stand a better chance of getting your money with my fiancé. Is that what this is all about?"

"The ransoms are incidental to our business in the region. Opportunities that arise must be exploited."

"How mercenary of you."

"I have to admit that I do not care about your opinion of me in the slightest, just that someone will pay for your release."

"If you must know, then yes."

Sarsosa nodded. "Then I shall appoint you facilities more suited to your station."

"And the rest of my expedition?"

"I have not yet decided their fate. Your behaviour shall, in part, determine what is to become of them."

"Your point is well taken. Do you mind if I ask you a question?"

"You may ask." Father Sarsosa leaned casually against his altar, arms folded across his chest.

"Does the Church condone what you are up to?"

"The Church? Oh. The vestments I wear. No, Miss Fiske, I am no longer with the Catholic Church, but I find their iconography projects a useful air of authority."

"You left the church?"

"I was excommunicated," he said.

"I suppose they look down on their missionaries turning mercenary."

"I was no missionary, and our disagreement was one of philosophy. Are you familiar with the writings of Charles Darwin?"

"On the Origin of the Species?"

Enthusiasm filled Father Sarsosa's voice. "Yes! The work changed my life. Darwin's true message was not one of biology, but one of leadership. Some men, you see, are simply superior to others. Smarter. Stronger. More suited to lead. More suited to set doctrine. I do not blame the Church for expelling me for my outspoken cries for modernisation; men of power must make what choices they must in order to secure their positions; I was a threat, and I was dealt with. So is the natural order."

"So you are no priest. Are you at least a military man?"

"After I left the church—"

"After they excommunicated you—"

"— I served my native Espania's army loyally, until my regiment was sent to Cuba during the rebellion. I saw an advantage in the guerrilla tactics that the natives used... an adaptability and flexibility the Spanish army lacked. A man must always be flexible to take opportunities as they arise. As soon as the Americans joined the Cubans, I defected with my most loyal soldiers and joined the revolution — together, we helped liberate Santiago. It was glorious."

"Impressive, I'm sure, but how does a revolutionary hero become a mercenary thug?"

Sarsosa raised an eyebrow. "You hope to rile me. Miss Fiske, you are a brave woman to have made your trip into the jungle. And either resourceful or lucky to have evaded my men until you entered the temple. It is circumstances like these — strife — that both reveal our highest selves and forge us into more perfect beings. You can rest assured... I shall not underestimate you."

Aldora blinked. "Nor I you, Commander."

"Then you must know that trying to get me to reveal more than I wish out of anger is foolish. But enough of me. The girl. She is yours?"

"The girl?"

He turned his head slightly. "The girl who followed you and the Indian. She has evaded my men, but we will have her soon. I'm not sure she's worth the trouble trying to take alive. Is she your daughter?"

"She is my ward," Aldora said carefully.

"Then she shall be returned to you intact."

"Thank you."

THE TOWER OF BABBAGE

"Show your thanks with your compliance, and you and your ward will remain safe. Take her away."

The guards separated Aldora and Amoxtli, taking the native hunter back towards the cell with the others, while Aldora was taken down another corridor.

They escorted her through a simple locked door into another cell. While still rather makeshift, this one was better appointed, with military-style cots and a folding table holding a bowl of fruit.

The engineer Mr. Kelley was sitting at the table, while a second, plumper man reclined on one of the cots. Both stood as she entered, remaining silent until the guards had shut the door.

"Are you alright, Miss Fiske?" the skinny man asked.

"None the worse for wear, Mr. Kelly." she said, turning to the larger fellow. "You are the director, Mr. Girnwood?"

The heavyset man raised a hand weakly. "And you are?"

"Miss Aldora Fiske." She walked up to Girnwood, stared him in the eyes for a second, then slapped him sharply across the face.

He rocked back, putting a hand on the wall to steady himself. "Wh-what?"

"That is for getting a good man killed."

"What?"

Aldora grabbed him by the tattered remains of his collar, slamming the man against the wall. "Henry Robinson was more of a man than you will ever know, you snivelling worm. He'd lived more, loved more, accomplished more than you can even dream, and now he's dead, leaving an orphaned daughter behind, all because you couldn't sit still and keep your mouth shut."

Girnwood gasped and grabbed at Aldora's fingers, trying to pry himself free. "The girl survived?"

"By all rights she is your responsibility now. Your lack of caution took her father from her, your self-importance almost took her life away, and I'd not add your incompetence to the burden she must bear for the rest of her life, but if you should survive this ordeal you must never forget what it is you've done. Are we clear, Mr Girnwood?"

"Y-yes, Miss Fiske."

"Excellent."

She gave the man a last shove against the wall, then released him and turned to sit at the table, pulling a banana from the bowl. Mr. Kelly and Mr. Girnwood exchanged glances.

"Did you know Mr. Robinson well?" Girnwood asked. "If so, I'm sorry for your—"

"Mr. Kelly." Aldora's quiet voice cut Girnwood's clumsy condolences off.

The engineer sat up straight. "Yes, Miss Fiske?"

She pointed the banana, half-peeled, at him. "The mercenaries have you examining the clockwork tower."

"Oh, yes. Fascinating thing."

"Is it Mayan?"

"Parts of it, yes."

"Only parts of it?"

"Well, yes. Others were, I believe, built by Mr. Babbage some decades ago when he visited the area."

"To what end?"

"Well, the Mayan clockwork, what remains, seems to be an observatory device of some sort. It measures wind, temperature, humidity, geothermic pressure... and the tower that Babbage constructed about it appears to be an Analytical Engine that interprets the presented data in a host of different ways. Taken together I believe it's sort of a predictive computation device."

"Predictive?"

"Oh yes. It's astoundingly complex. Babbage built a machine that can predict the outcome of almost any human action, given accurate variables."

"What does Sarsosa want with it? He seems more a man of action than computations and fortune-telling."

Mr. Kelly seemed uncomfortable. "Well, the original purpose of the device was to predict the effects of human endeavour. The Commander wants me to alter it so that you can start from a desired outcome and work out the steps necessary to get to that point."

Aldora gasped. "Is that... possible?"

"Sarsosa believes so. And it is. In theory. But I'm just one man... it'll take months, if not years, to make the changes he wants."

The door opened with a scraping sound, and all three of the prisoners froze.

Rough hands shoved Penny through the doorway, and the young girl stumbled, almost falling.

Aldora was next to her in an instant. "Are you alright?"

"Scuffed up a bit," Penny said. "Lead the guards on a merry chase around and through the clockworks, I did. Hello, Mr.Girnwood. Is my father here?"

Girnwood's face fell and he sagged against the wall. "Ahem. Well. Penelope. You see..."

Aldora knelt next to the girl, eyes glassy, hand on her arm and shoulder.

THE TOWER OF BABBAGE

Later, when the crying had stopped, the two girls sat in the cell's corner. Aldora had asked the guards for, and received, a stiff bristled brush that she was using to try and de-tangle Penny's auburn hair. Her own hand strayed intermittently to touch her own scarlet locks, bound back in a bun the best she could manage.

"Father always said that he'd be gone some day," Penny said softly, breaking the silence. "That I had to be ready."

"He was a brave man who frequently put himself in dangerous circumstances."

"He did his best to keep me safe."

"I know, child."

"But it isn't a safe world, is it, Miss Fiske?"

Aldora didn't answer right away, and the gentle rasping of the brush through Penny's hair filled the room.

"What do you know of your mother?"

"Most of the time father said that she died in childbirth." Penny's voice was flat, emotionless. "But sometimes, when he was well in his cups, he'd say that she'd left us instead. I think he said that she died to spare my feelings."

"Perhaps."

"That's silly though," Penny said. "How can you have feelings about someone you've never known? The woman who birthed me... she's nothing more than a bedtime story."

"Some say the bond between a mother and child extends beyond simple association."

"Do you think so?"

Aldora brushed silently before answering. "Not in my experience. I've seen stronger bonds between adoptive parents and children than I ever felt for my own."

"I'm sorry you didn't at least have a father like mine."

"No one had a father like yours," Aldora said. "We'll not see the likes of Henry Robinson again, and the world is poorer for it."

"What will become of me?" Penny said. "If we escape, that is. I don't have godparents."

"We will get through this."

Penny sighed. "It doesn't seem likely."

Aldora turned the girl so that they were facing one another. "Penelope Robinson, I give you my word as a Lady that we will get through this. We will escape. And when we return to London, I will take you into my household as if... as if you were my own."

"You will?" Penny's voice sounded very small.

"I... owed your father. I owed him much, and now that he has passed, it is a debt that I will never be able to repay. Raising his daughter is the best way I can respect his memory."

"Thank you, Miss Fiske."

"We've been risking our lives together, Penny. Please, call me Aldora."

The girl threw her arms around the slender woman, who, after her initial surprise, returned the embrace.

Behind them Mr. Girnwood cleared his throat noisily. Aldora levelled a cool gaze in his direction, not yet letting go of the girl.

"That's a touching display of affection and I for one am very moved," the director said. "If only I had my camera. Such emotion."

"What do you want, Mr. Girnwood?"

He seemed hesitant. "It seems to me that it would be far easier to simply let ourselves be ransomed. Safer, at any rate, and I'm sure that you'd rather not risk the girl in an escape attempt."

"As I am sure you recall, Penelope's father was murdered." Aldora let Penny go and shifted in her seat to face the man. "He was a good friend of mine for many years. This is not a wrong I can let go unavenged."

"Me neither," Penny said.

"Surely the authorities—"

"Commander Sarsosa is constructing a powerful analytic engine capable of crafting plans with inhuman precision," Aldora said. "If it's as effective as Mr. Kelly indicates, then once it's complete it'll account for the efforts of the authorities."

"Yes, but—"

"Have you spoken to the Commander, Mr. Girnwood?"

"You know I have."

"What is your impression of the man?"

"He's a hard man. Cruel, perhaps."

"Ambitious. Ruthless. But what struck me was something he said, something about strife and conflict bringing out the best in mankind. Tell me, if you had the almost godlike omniscience of this Babbage Tower, what would you do with it, Mr. Girnwood?"

"Oh, well, I suppose I'd use it to make the world a better place?"

"You would. Most people would. But your ideal world is not mine, and Commander Sarsosa's ideal world, I would hazard, is not anyone's."

The director fell silent.

"We must remove him from power by what means we can, for after he completes his machine, he will be a god, and no one can oppose him."

"Mr. Kelly can simply refuse—"

"I will!"

"Mr. Kelly can refuse, be executed, and be replaced by engineers more amicable to serving a monster like Sarsosa. There are, no doubt, plenty in the guild."

"There are," Mr. Kelly agreed.

"But why does it fall to us?" the director whined.

"Because we can. Because we're here, at the right time, in the right place. We will be the last random variable in the engine's calculations, Mr. Girnwood. Humanity's last chance to evade the controlling grasp of a megalomaniac. We will stop him, because we must."

"And because the bastard killed my father," Penny said.

"Penelope!"

"I said 'dastard'."

"You were correct the first time," Aldora said.

"Well and good," the director said. "I defer to your superior logic, and your need to see Henry avenged. But how do you propose we go about wreaking such vengeance, stuck in this cell as we are?"

"Maybe I could fake an illness and we could lure the guards in?" Mr. Kelly suggested.

"You've been reading a few too many penny dreadfuls." Girnwood frowned.

"Penny Dreadfuls. Ooh, I like that," Penny said. "And I'm the dreadful one with the key, aren't I?"

She opened her hand, revealing a small iron key.

"Wherever did you get that?" the engineer asked.

"Nicked it when they pinched me."

Aldora took the key from Penny's hand. "It's a skeleton key."

She walked to the cell door, stooping to look through the keyhole. "It looks like it'll fit. And I don't see any guards in the hall."

"They're probably at the evening meal," Mr. Kelly said. "Every night Sarsosa gathers his men and has a small religious service."

"Mercenaries with religion, what next?" Girnwood shook his head.

"It doesn't last long."

"Then we need to move quickly." Aldora unlocked the door, wincing at its loud click.

She handed the key back to Penny. "Head back to the cell where the others are being kept and bring them to the escape tunnel."

Penny handed the key to Mr. Kelly. "No, I want to go with you."

"Do as I say. I can handle Father Sarsosa, but not if I'm worrying about you."

A small sad smile spread across the girl's face. "You sound like father."

Aldora paused, then held the girl close again. "He will not go unavenged."

"Come with us," Girnwood said, pausing in the doorway as he left, following Kelly. "Forget vengeance and Sarsosa."

"This isn't just about revenge," Aldora said, nudging Penny gently after the men. "You've heard what this Babbage tower can do. I can't let it stay in the hands of an opportunistic dictator like that. He'll set the world aflame and think himself a saint for it."

Girnwood backed away, out the open door, followed shortly by Mr. Kelley.

"Go, Penny. Be safe. I'll come for you."

Penny bit her lip and nodded, slipping out after the director.

It didn't take Aldora long to find the makeshift chapel where Father Jago Sarsosa was preaching to his men. She followed the booming tenor of his voice to the large pavilion tent.

She daren't approach the tent itself, but through the candlelit shadows she could clearly see the mercenary commander making broad sweeping gestures near his makeshift altar, the silhouettes of his men in rows of folding chairs watching his every motion.

"Some of you come from our native Spain," he said, preaching in English. "Others joined us after our liberation in Cuba, or after, when we travelled to Columbia. Some have asked me, Father Sarsosa, why did you delay and extend the conflict in Columbia? Why did you use your position as a trusted revolutionary to stymie the cause of freedom and drag things on further?"

"I will say to you all, that my cause, that God's cause, is not freedom. What the revolutionaries call 'freedom' is just a lack of discipline. I have always preached more discipline, and no institution better impresses discipline upon a people than a strong military, and when is a military at its strongest?"

"WAR!" The reply from his guards was so sudden, so forceful, that Aldora had to steel herself against bolting.

"War!" Sarsosa continued. "War brings out the best in men. It creates circumstances where superior men rise to the top, and weak leaders are cast down to shatter on the Earth.

"It was for this reason that we accepted the Cartel's contract to bring war to Russia. I do not care for the Russian people, they are not my people, but they, too, are deserving of war.

"It was in St. Petersburg that I learnt my lesson that one does not need to pitch battle to incite war. It was Hernandez — stand, Hernandez — it

THE TOWER OF BABBAGE

was one round from Hernandez's rifle that turned protest and riot into rebellion on the steps of the palace. One man died, and what was born from the blood that Hernandez spilt?"

"WAR!"

"And now, while we hid in the jungles, asked by the Cartel to do the same for Mexico, what has God brought us? This machine. With this machine we can accomplish our great task, our holy feat, the ignition of a world-wide perpetual conflict that will sweep across Europe. This machine will tell us whose death will ignite this eternal flame, and how we can best position ourselves to benefit from it. This will be a great war. An unending war. The last war to end all wars. One shot will ring out, and then what will we have?"

"WAR!" came the echoed chorus. "WAR! WAR! WAR!"

Sickened, Aldora retreated back into the ruins.

Things were more dire than she had feared. Sarsosa's motives were not selfish. He didn't want to enrich himself.

He was the worst sort of idealist, one convinced that bloodshed would elevate humanity, and his charisma had allowed him to sway his men to a similar fanaticism. He'd blended his authoritarian militarism with the trappings of religion into a perfect nightmare fusion of theocratic fascism.

She crept to the foot of the clockwork tower, stopping to gather up a pair of 8 lb kegs of cordite, one under each arm.

Unlike Mr. Kelly she was no engineer, and knew nothing of the device's workings or its structural integrity, and she was no military demolitions expert either. Still, she did the best she could, secreting kegs of artillery powder around the tower's base in out of the way places, small trails of black grit leading back to its centre, where a thicker trail lead away from the base.

The Mayans and Mr. Babbage had left human-sized passages through the workings so that engineers could reach the machine's innermost guts, and Aldora wove powder trails to kegs hidden deep within.

"Stop her!"

Aldora had just placed her eighth keg when Sarsosa and his men returned to the central chamber. At the priest's cry, one of his men took a knee, shouldered his rifle, and fired in one smooth motion, the heat from the round's passage caressing the side of her neck. She ducked aside, back into the shelter of the clockwork mechanism.

"*Idiota!*" Sarsosa pulled his pistol and shot the kneeling mercenary in the temple. "Don't risk the tower. Kill the woman if you must, but preserve the mechanism!"

The soldiers swarmed towards the tower, leaving their dead comrade by Sarsosa's feet.

Aldora retreated to the centre of the machine and began climbing, using its brass pipes and steel rods as hand-holds. The soldiers ran up the scaffolding, entering the tower above and below her, some with machetes or knives in hand.

A grasping hand reached through the network of pipes towards her, and she grabbed it by the fingers, twisting them until they broke with a loud snap. Their owner fell screaming.

Down below another mercenary, climbing up after her, swiped at her ankle with his machete, missing by mere inches. She let her grip go and dropped half-a-foot to plant her heel squarely between his eyes; he fell with a yell to collide with the man below him as she continued her ascent.

Aldora climbed until she was level with the highest scaffolding at the peak of the tower.

A nearly out-of-breath Russian mercenary was thundering up the ramp towards her, serrated knife in hand, twisted grimace on his scarred face. She pulled a wooden rod from the scaffold just in time to parry a vicious swipe, returning a clumsy riposte that impacted sharply with the man's breastbone. She adjusted her grip to account for the stick's weight and balance.

When the man next slashed his blade at her face she struck his wrist with the flat of the stick, shattering the joint, then jabbed the flat end of it into his throat.

The Russian fell to his knees, gasping and holding his trachea. Aldora calmly retrieved the pistol from his hip-holster, then shoved him off the top of the tower with the pad of her foot, watching with quiet satisfaction as he tumbled to the stone floor below.

More mercenaries climbed, converging to trap her at the top.

Aldora picked up the Russian's dropped knife and used it to quickly cut the twine binding the long vertical pole from the scaffolding nearest her, then swung down to wrap her arms and legs around its length. Her momentum carried it away from the tower, twine further down its length snapping as the weight strained it. She rode the falling pole until it lodged against the far wall, the impact almost jarring the strength from her limbs.

"Get her!" Sarsosa cried. "She's away from the machine — shoot her!"

Aldora hung by her knees from the pole, hem of her tunic trapped between her thighs, bending backwards at the waist until she was fully inverted, aiming the Russian's pistol at one of the gunpowder kegs near the tower's base.

Mercenaries braced their rifles against the tower's pipes, rods, and levers, taking aim and firing, their deadly rounds impacting the limestone blocks around Aldora. She shut out the danger, shut out the distraction, closed one eye, aimed, and pulled the trigger.

THE TOWER OF BABBAGE

Explosion.
Falling.
Impact.
Pain.
Black.
Get up.
Get up.

Aldora had only blacked out for a moment.

When her senses returned she was deaf save for a powerful ringing in her ears, and at first the blackness made her fear blindness as well.

Bereft of her two primary senses, Aldora stumbled through a dark abyss, feeling only the pain of what was probably a broken arm and smelling the potent mixture of spent cordite, scorched brass, and burning flesh. Her good arm extended its hand to help her navigate as she crawled over ruined debris.

As her eyes adjusted she noted a dim glow from small pockets of burning refuse, providing enough light to see by. The concussive force of the explosion had damaged the temple's structure and it was in danger of collapse. Many of the tunnels leading away from the central chamber had already crumbled, including the one leading outside.

She turned from it, making her way towards the passage leading to the Mayan escape tunnel.

Her sense of hearing began to return slowly, first with a hollow echoing that eventually resolved itself into a single shouted word.

"FISKE!"

It was Jago Sarsosa. Somehow he had survived the explosion.

"FISKE!"

He sounded maddened, whether from the pain or from the rage at being thwarted.

There was a low bass boom followed by a crack. Sarsosa was shooting at her.

Aldora looked over her shoulder to see the fallen priest shambling in pursuit. His face looked masked in crimson, his hair jagged with stiffening blood, one eye bright with anger, the other gone dark. He was limping, but not exactly slowly, one shaking hand levelling a pistol in her direction.

He fired again, missing by inches only because of his loss of depth perception. He was adjusting quickly.

Aldora turned and crawled over the debris as fast as her broken arm allowed. Her legs were uninjured but she found it hard to focus, hard to move quickly.

"I am concussed," she said conversationally, her voice distant and cloudy in her ears.

She staggered sideways down the corridor leading to the ancient escape tunnel, a bullet impacting where her head had been moments before.

Aldora reached the ladder down, slowly but carefully navigating it one-handed, her balance still off. She misjudged one of the middle rungs and fell to the ground below, jarring her shattered shoulder and giving out an involuntary cry.

Sarsosa leapt down from above, sturdy boots landing next to her, pistol in hand. His left knee buckled but he did not fall, a grimace distorting his lips, blood dripping from his ruined eye, down his cheek, to fall upon his waistcoat. What she could make out through the dull light filtering from above was horrific.

"*Mato usted*," he managed through gritted teeth, bringing his pistol to bear.

Aldora lashed out with her foot, the ball of her toe kicking the gun out of his hand. It fell into the electrified battery pond with a crackling spark, lightning dancing along the metal casing even as it sank, illuminating their struggle from below.

"*Mato con mis manos!*"

Sarsosa lunged faster than the concussed gentlewoman could react, his powerful calloused hands wrapping around Aldora's slender neck.

A greyness came to her already fading vision as he cut off the oxygen supply to her lungs, literally choking the life out of her.

Her one good hand flailed uselessly at his arm, unable to reach his face or neck, until, her will fading, it fell to rest on the pool's bank. Her fingertips touched sharp flint.

Almost instinctively, her fingers closed around it, finding a bit of broken shaft, the tip of a spear skipped across an electric pond hours earlier.

Summoning the last of her will, the last of her strength, Aldora gripped the spearhead firmly before driving it around, up and into Sarsosa's remaining eye. He screamed and let go of her neck, his hands flying to his ruined face, legs kicking in agony for the time it took the woman to regain her breath.

By the time she had recovered, he was still.

Aldora stared at the dead Spaniard for a long moment, until the light from his sparking gun had finally faded away, leaving her in absolute blackness.

"Henry," she whispered, leaning her head back against the tunnel wall. It would be so easy to let go, now. To let the rumbling in the stone against her back lure her down into oblivion, to give up the finger-hold she had onto life, to let herself slip away into the comforting stillness of death. She had fought hard. She had won. She had defeated Father Sarsosa and avenged the murder of her lost love. She had kept her promise to Penelope.

Most of her promise.

Penny was alone, now, without a parent. She faced a life alone as an urchin, or toiling away in a work-house, if she ever made it back to England. Lord only knew what dangers orphans faced here in Mexico. The girl needed her, and she'd given her the hope of a stable life. She'd given her word. As appealing as the peace of death felt, Aldora had given her word, and she was a Lady of her word.

"Penelope," she whispered, summoning all her will. She stood, bracing herself against the wall to rise, next to the dead Spaniard.

There was one obstacle left in her way. She stood at the edge of the deadly pool she could no longer see, then strode to the back of her side of the pond.

Four paces.

About eight to ten feet.

Her flagging endurance would have to suffice.

Aldora tensed for but a moment, then sprang forward, bare feet flying across limestone until she judged herself at the edge of the pool, then leapt.

"I would never have dreamed that a mere woman could accomplish so much destruction," the Colonel said.

The escaped captives crouched in the jungle at the edge of Zipactonal's clearing, watching the last few standing pillars of stone collapse into the ruin.

"A remarkable woman, even for a Fiske," Carvel said. "I daresay in the mould of Queen Victoria herself. We'll not see her like again."

"She's not dead," Penny said, stepping forward. "She can't be!"

"Capable she may have been," Carvel said, "but no one could have survived that."

"She could!" Penny turned burying her face in Amotzxil's tunic. "Aldora's too... she can't be dead!"

Kelley looked away awkwardly.

"She... she's all I have."

Amoxtli started, then pointed towards the ruins. "*Xchúupal! 'U'uyeh!*"

A shambling figure became visible in the smoke and dust, stopping and abruptly straightening as it neared the periphery. A warm wind blew across the clearing, revealing the bedraggled but distinct form of Miss Aldora Fiske. She was limping, one arm hung limply at her side, and her face was bloodied, but the gentlewoman was very much alive.

The adults watched in shock as Aldora approached, only young Penny breaking ranks to throw herself bodily into the ragged woman. She caught her gingerly, no trace of pain crossing her face as she held the sobbing child.

Her eyes sought out the Colonel, steady, clear, challenging.

The man looked away.

"Is this where I'll be living?" Penny looked up at the Fiske townhouse. She didn't have much luggage, just a few outfits that the girls had picked up in Mérida before their trip back to London.

"Impressed?" Aldora asked. She'd acquired new clothing as well, pleased with the availability of European-style garments in the Mexican port city, only a few seasons out of date.

"It's nice." Penny was good at sounding polite but unimpressed. "Not as nice as a Maharajah's palace of course, but it'll do."

Aldora adjusted her parasol, hiding her smile. "I am ever so pleased that it meets with your approval."

Penny smoothed out the unfamiliar lacy hem of her skirt. "I've never... lived in a house, you know. Father and I... we always kept moving, staying with others. I've never had a home."

The townhouse's door opened to emit Aldora's fiancé Bartleby. He flashed the girls a grin.

Aldora rolled her eyes. "Penelope, this is my fiancé, Alton Bartleby. Mr. Bartleby has a home of his own, though you wouldn't realise it from how often you'll find him here."

"Penny," the girl said, giving a small curtsy.

"It's a pleasure to make your acquaintance, Miss Robinson," Alton said. He stepped aside, revealing a young Chinese girl in a short sleeved dress. "Allow me to introduce to you Miss Xin Yang, ward of my business partner."

"你是我的朋友？" The Chinese girl stepped forward with a friendly smile.

Penny blinked with pleasant surprise, then responded in Xin Yang's own tongue. "是的！我成最好的朋友！"

She turned to Aldora. "She wants to be friends!"

"I know." Aldora stepped aside towards her fiancé. "I understand Mandarin. Why don't you two run off to the yard? Xin Yang can show you

THE TOWER OF BABBAGE

around the grounds."

Penny dropped her small bag and ran off, hand-in-hand, with the other girl.

Aldora turned to Alton. "You did that on purpose."

"Did what?" Alton asked. "I simply thought that your new foster might enjoy someone her own age to play with while adjusting to her new household."

"Nothing you think is simple."

"And if you should happen to decide that a more permanent stewardship of Xin Yang might be occasionally a benefit..."

Aldora laughed. "Does James know you're here?"

"Oh good lord no. He prefers to have the girl in our own home, even though he never leaves his workshop. The chap can be a bit... overprotective at times."

"He's protective of the both of you."

Bartleby rolled his eyes. "Don't I know it. It's tiresome. Anyway, I'm pleased to see that you've reconsidered how children fit into your lifestyle."

"It's not a matter of children, it's family," Aldora said. "We all have them; most people have two. The family's we're born into, and the families we choose. It's only by way of rare accident that the two happen to coincide."

Bartleby watched the two girls disappear around the corner of the house. "And which is this Penelope?"

"Whatever the matter of the former, she is firmly the latter. I have chosen that she be raised in my home, as my daughter. I trust, dear fiancé, that you do not object?"

"I wouldn't dare."

MICHAEL COORLIM

FINE YOUNG TURKS

Aldora Fiske navigated the shifting patterns of the quadrille effortlessly. Her evening gown was cut was to the very edge of fashion, a diaphanous teal tunic over her draped narrow pastel blue skirt, waistline cinched high just below the bust in a precise Empire style, her hemline just above the cuff of her high curved heels. To the untrained eye her movements were casual, effortless, and relaxed, but there was purpose behind every step, intent behind every turn, a reason behind every change in partners. There were many she would speak with this evening, many she would listen to, and it was the shuffling steps of the quadrille which would bring dancers together and take them apart again.

The band played on, Turks with European orchestral instruments, playing with precision and largely ignorant of the subtle conflict filling the Constantinople palace's ballroom around them, the dancers an international sea of muted European style amid opulent Ottoman decor.

Her partners in these movements were almost as adept at this social chess as she, and everyone had their own political agenda for the evening. None were so inexperienced that an unexpected twist would trip them up or make them lose their pace, and so the lunges and feints of this dance were intended to channel individuals towards and away from one another, as desired. The experienced players, such as Aldora herself, knew how to think several movements and motions ahead. The game became one of understanding and anticipating the choices in partner other dancers were apt to make, and then presenting attractive alternatives to get them where you wanted them to be.

Having finished flirting with the eligible and noble Italian Comte Montagni, Aldora moved with the changing measure, displacing Mme Viviani, wife of the French Minister of Labour.

She smiled as her movements began to mirror those of her new partner, the wealthy industrialist Brugmann. "Only in Constantinople would I dream to see a French woman dancing with a German."

Brugmann laughed. "Perhaps the atmosphere puts us in a conciliatory mood, Miss Fiske. It is yet Miss, is it not?"

"I do approach the end of my spinsterhood," she said. "But you needn't fear my fiance minding my dancing with another man."

"A trusting man, your Mr.Bartleby. And you trust him enough to travel half the world away."

"If the Reich can trust the Third Republic..."

"It isn't France that concerns us, but their chosen ally."

The dance had brought Minister Guignard Viviani himself alongside the couple, no doubt a manoeuvre the Frenchman had initiated soon after seeing his wife dancing with the industrialist, and had been compelled to complete even after she had moved on.

"You needn't concern yourself with the Tsar," he said in passing. "Russia is in no position to initiate a war, not after the trouncing the Japanese gave them."

"If they're so weak an ally, then why waste your time courting them?" Brugmann asked.

Guignard smirked and the dance shifted, Aldora moving to join him.

"As a counterweight to your own ambitions, of course," he said. "The French and Russian governments are not inclined to start a war, but you can rest assured that together we are well equipped to end one."

"I'm sure you find great pleasure in rattling your sabres," Aldora said, subtly moving the Frenchman away from the German, "but I can assure you that none here are impressed."

"Forgive me, of course," the Frenchman said.

"It is from our elusive host that you should beg forgiveness."

"Ah! Perhaps the opportunity is upon me."

Guignard turned slightly, allowing Aldora a glimpse of the curtained archway leading into the ballroom. A handsome Turk stood there, dressed in a long emerald robe with tight sleeves over a pale blue and navy tunic. He was tall and thin, with an olive cast to his features that Aldora found quite appealing. The dance's steps turned her away from the man, and far be it from her to make a scene craning her neck around for him.

"Our host joins us," Guignard said. "Cemal Yavuzade Bey."

"What do you know of the man?" she asked, careful to keep her interest sounding mild.

FINE YOUNG TURKS

"He's a representative of the Ottoman Empire's ruling Committee of Union and Progress parliamentary party."

"A mouthful of a label."

"Perhaps you've heard of them by their other name, the Young Turks?"

"That does sound familiar. I remember hearing something about a coup?"

"From what I can recall the Young Turks marched on the Sultan and demanded he reinstate the constitution he'd suspended. The man capitulated, and the Turks seized power. This ball is most likely a calculated ploy by the Committee to show off the empire's reforms to the great powers of Europe, to inspire confidence in the "Sick Old Man of Europe's" financial future."

Aldora chuckled. "For a transparent ploy to inspire confidence in ones debtors, it certainly is a pleasant one."

While she had expected spectacle at the ball — the familiar European style was a considerate touch — she did not expect their host to be so young and handsome. As the dance progressed and she passed from Guignard to a new partner she spared Cemal a second glance — and to her fluster he caught it, deep hazel eyes locking her own pale blue. She found it impossible to look away from their intensity at first, and when she finally managed found herself partnered with Mr. Herbert, the loathsome American industrialist whose great airship had brought most of her fellow guests all the way to Asia.

"Miss Fiske!" His greedy eyes sought out her décolletage. "How delightful it is to have the opportunity to dance with you."

"Forgive me, Mr. Herbert. I do feel a bit faint. You will excuse me?" She backed away, still moving in time to the music but increasing the distance between herself and her temporary partner.

Mr. Herbert nodded but frowned, finding himself alone in the quadrille. He made a game attempt to dance with an invisible partner for a few movements, then walked awkwardly off the floor to titters just loud enough for him to hear.

Aldora swayed between dancing couples, away from the centre of the ballroom, instinctively navigating between their complex steps as easily as when she had been part of the pattern herself. Cool air across her flushed skin drew her through a tapered arch onto a vast balcony, and she chided herself for having had such a public reaction. It was unthinkable for a lady of her stature to show such obvious interest. She could but hope the ballroom's lighting was such that none noticed her blush, her gaze, her obvious stare.

She leaned against the balcony, letting the cool Mediterranean breeze soothe her embarrassment, and looked out over Constantinople's skyline, its domes and towers silhouetted against the setting sun. Black shapes silhouetted against the fading light, passing between the minarets, both European airships and the smaller Turkish ornithopters with their articulated wings, the distant lights of their swaying, darting movements almost seeming like fireflies one might reach out and grasp.

"Would you like to go for a ride?"

She'd never heard the Bey speak, but she knew it was his voice without turning around. She daren't. "I beg your pardon?"

"You're watching the ornithopters. I'm told they never took hold in Northern Europe... my personal 'thopter sits on the roof of this palace. Perhaps you'd like to take a ride in it some time?"

"Thank you for the offer," Aldora said. "But I was merely enjoying the view."

"Do you like it?"

"It's breathtaking."

"Tell me," he said, standing next to her. "Tell me what you see."

She spared him a sideways look, fixating on the inches between their hands on the railing. "I see the setting sun. The rising moon. I see the bay, and ships of all sorts."

"The harbour is the Golden Horn, and across the Bosporus Strait is Stamboul, the Byzantium of the Greeks and Constantinople of the Romans."

"I thought this palace was in Constantinople."

Cemal chuckled. "It is. Stamboul is the old city, the old way, built on seven hills, each topped with an extravagant mosque by Sultans gone by. On this side of the bay is Pera. Both are Constantinople, but Stamboul is its past. Pera is its future. Pera is what I've invited you all here to see."

"What makes Pera its future?" Aldora glanced at her host, caught him looking at her, and looked away quickly.

"Pera exists on the cusp of Europe and Asia," he said. "The embassies are here. The trading houses of Europe have their offices here. On the streets of Pera you might think yourself in any of the great cities of England or France, with just a taste of what makes Constantinople Turkish. On its streets you will pass citizens from across the Empire, from Egypt to Macedonia to Kuwait to Armenia."

"It sounds wonderfully cosmopolitan." Somehow her hand had moved closer to his, and she could almost feel the heat radiating from his skin.

"As the empire has been for centuries."

"Cemal Bey?"

The gruff voice startled Aldora, and she stepped quickly away from Cemal. One of his servants — or guards — waited in the doorway. "*Sizin misafirler sizi soruyor.*"

"*Ben hemen orada olacaktır.*" He turned to face Aldora straight on, and she found herself almost lost in the deep hazel of his eyes. "If you will excuse me?"

"Yes," she said. "Of course."

Aldora stayed, waiting on the balcony, watching the airships drift above the harbour long after her host had left.

"There you are." Penelope, her eleven year-old ward, stomped towards her, her white skirts bunched in her hands, broad velvet sash around her middle.

"Have you been behaving yourself?" Aldora asked, taking a moment to compose herself, hands flying lightly to her hair.

"I'm being a Lady," Penny said. "I was wondering if we might go visit Kalil tomorrow."

"Your friend. He lives across the bay, in Stamboul?"

Penny nodded. "Yes, in the Aksaray neighbourhood. I know the way. I can show you."

"Perhaps," Aldora said. "I would like to see more of the city."

"Kalil and I can serve as your guides," Penny said. "Father and I visited the city often."

The girl's smile faded slightly, and she turned to overlook the city alongside her guardian.

"I miss Father."

"I know you do, dear." Aldora slipped an arm around the girl's shoulder. "I miss him as well. Henry... he was one of the finest men I've had the pleasure of knowing."

Taking care of Henry Robinson's daughter was the only way she could make things right with herself. She'd arrived too late to save him from the Spanish madman who'd taken his life in the jungles of Mexico, but she had rescued the girl. Adopting her was the closest she would get to reconciliation with the girl's father. It would have to be enough.

"Let's return indoors," Aldora said. "It should be almost supper."

The girls turned and headed back towards the ballroom. A tall woman — lean and graceful, with dark black skin and dark amber eyes, mahogany hair tied in a long braid, dressed in simple but elegant sleeveless silk vest over a long layered tunic — met them at the archway.

"Miss Fiske?" she asked.

"Yes?"

"I am Safiyya, Cemal Bey's *uşak*."

"An *uşak* is a valet," Penny whispered.

"The Ottomans have female valets?" Aldora asked.

"The Young Turk's reforms allow women to do many things that before we could not," Safiyya said. "Cemal Bey wishes your company at his table for supper."

Aldora smiled brightly at the unexpected news. "You may of course relay to him that we accept."

Safiyya looked down at Aldora's ward. "The invitation was but for one, but I am sure he would not object—"

"No, that's okay." Penny gave Aldora a sly grin. "You needn't concern yourself with me. I can entertain myself while you entertain the Bey."

"Penelope!"

Penny's grin only widened. Safiyya chuckled.

"This is what now?" Brugmann sniffed at the clear liquid the palace servants had set before him. "An aperitif? It smells of anise. I thought your Muslim faith forbade you alcohol?"

Brugmann sat to Cemal's left, across from Aldora, who counted herself fortunate to be seated next to the handsome Turk. Mme Viviani sat on Aldora's right, next to her husband, who himself was across the round table from the Italian aristocrat Comte Montagni, and the American industrialist Herbert.

"It's *rakı*," Cemal poured a measure of cold water into his drink, turning it from transparent to a milky white. "I can assure you, Mr. Brugmann, the reformist government is a secularist one... but even before the revolution, the different religious communities had their own laws. Allah's restrictions are for those who choose to follow the Prophet."

"And you yourself drink?" Aldora asked.

Cemal smiled at her. "I've always been a secularist, particularly where it comes to fine drink."

The table's samite cloth was laden with a variety of small dishes served in delicate porcelain bowls. Aldora had sampled a grainy-looking salty white cheese which she found similar to feta, a slice of ripe melon she did not care for, and what had turned out to be a pepper and walnut paste straddling the cusp of heat and pain.

"I've heard told the Young Turk movement sprung from dissatisfied academics," she said.

"*Oui*," Minister Viviani said. "The founding members were students of the *Académie de Machination* in Paris."

"The Committee is eternally grateful to the government of France for their compliance," Cemal said.

"France has always supported progressive causes." Mme Viviani picked up a slender skewer from the appetisers arrayed out before the guests, nibbling at the olive on the end.

"As you did so elegantly in Morocco." Brugmann sipped a thick golden yogurt from a small shallow dish.

The Labour Minister's wife visibly bristled, pointing the end of her skewer at the German industrialist.

"You know as well as any the only scandal in Morocco was Germany's," Aldora said, wiping the corners of her mouth with a napkin. "Though Britain thanks you for the opportunity to come to France's defence. I doubt the *Entente Cordiale* would be as strong as it is without you providing us the opportunity to test our alliance."

Brugmann's brow furrowed. "Pfah! What does a woman understand of the nuances of geopolitics?"

"We know enough to see Germany's bluster is just despair that they've entered the great empire building game too late." Viviani's piercing laughter echoed through the banquet chamber. "What will your Kaiser do? Where will you find your colonies? There is not world enough left for a German Empire. There are no more Africas. No more Americas. You trail behind England and France, begging for scraps of China, but we all know that the Reich will not be satisfied with what diplomacy acquires!"

Brugmann's face reddened, his hands clenching into fists. Safiyya half-rose out of her seat, only to be stopped by a small gesture from Cemal. The room held its collective breath.

"Germany will not start a war," Aldora spoke quietly, her voice enormous in the silence. "In politics we speak in rhetoric, but you must acknowledge that the Kaiser and his Chancellor are no less reasonable men than your President and his senate, Mme Viviani. And reasonable men must recognise that the age of war is one that Europe has left behind. We, the people of the United Kingdom, the Republic of France, the Empire of Germany, the Kingdom of Italy, and the twin kingdoms of Austria-Hungary... we are no longer warriors. We are consumers. We are people of business, and the economic realities of trade limit the viability of combat. War, gentlemen, is no longer a profitable enterprise."

Brugmann stared at the gentlewoman in silence for several heartbeats before breaking out into genuine laughter. He sat back into his chair and the others at Cemal's table relaxed slightly, some lapsing into nervous chuckles themselves.

"Eloquent as always, Miss Fiske." The German returned his gaze to the food laid out before them. "I have heard these same sentiments from many, even in my own Empire... but you are a civilian, an aristocrat, and an academic — what know you of the ways of war? Forgive me if I find you a trifle naive."

He paused, gaze flickering to Cemal. "No offence to the academics in the room, esteemed Bey. And forgive me my outburst."

"I take no offence," Cemal said. "I do not discourage spirited — if civil — debate. But I am no academic. I came to the Committee by military means."

"You were a military man?" Mr. Herbert asked, pausing, rice-stuffed vine leaf half-way to his lips.

"Naval," Cemal said. "The Sultan never trusted the Navy or its Admirals, so our airship fleet consisted of one vessel. As the man agitating most vocally for the modernisation of our military, I was honoured with its command. You can imagine my dismay when I discovered we were never to leave port. When the Committee came to solicit aid in their coup, offering a vision of military reform... well, how could I refuse?"

"Please do not take this the wrong way," the Italian Comte Montagni said, "but what of your military oaths? I do not mean to insult, but I have difficulty reconciling the notion of an honourable revolutionary who betrays his word."

Cemal took a small sip of rakı. "I take my oaths seriously, but I made my vow to the Empire, not to the Sultan. I joined the Young Turk movement because I believe that its reforms — secularisation, modernisation, and the restoration of the constitution — are what is best for the peoples of the Empire."

"Well put," Aldora said. "Bravo."

"And you, Miss Fiske?" Cemal said. "Tell me of yourself."

"She is a Fiske," Brugmann didn't look up as he dipped a wedge of bread into chickpea mash. "What else is there to know?"

Aldora coloured.

"I am afraid I don't get your meaning," Cemal said.

"She comes from a very old and aristocratic family," Mme Viviani said. "One of the few old houses that have managed to retain its wealth as well as its social standing."

"I must admit that the invitations were sent out to influential Europeans by Committee members better versed in Europe's great families than I," Cemal said, "but I am glad that you were able to join us."

Aldora bowed her head slightly. "My father, regretfully, was unable to make the trip, and sent me in his stead." That was a lie.

The invitation had never come to the attention of her father. It had been mistakenly delivered to her town-house rather than the family country estate, and she had seized upon the opportunity to take a trip to Asia before her wedding of necessity.

"This is an excellent cheese," Comte Montagni said. "Feta?"

"*Beyaz peynir*," Safiyya said. "Very similar, but this is a native Turkish curd."

"I quite enjoy the music," Mme Viviani said, turning to regard the musicians, one seated with a narrow trapezoidal zither, the other plucking a long-necked lute, playing a constant soft accompaniment. "It's very non-intrusive."

"It's an improvisational *fasıl*," Cemal said.

"Improvisational?" Herbert said. "I suppose after paying for the feast laid out before us, you couldn't afford anything better."

"I don't get your meaning."

Brugmann snorted. "American improvisational music is entertainment for the working class. How quickly Herr Herbert forgets that Beethoven and Mozart were fond of extemporaneous compositions. You have heard of Beethoven, Mr. Herbert?"

The American stammered until Mme Viviani interrupted him. "You speak as if you find an inferiority in the people."

"Inferiority? No. Let's call it a commonality."

"Don't underestimate the significance of the workers," Aldora said.

"You needn't lecture me," Brugmann said. "Even in Germany our *Sozialdemokratische Partei* radicals are quickly becoming a majority party. Be glad, Miss Fiske, that your own land's unions are more moderate."

"I'm afraid labour politics are not my forte," Aldora said.

"A dangerous ignorance, if you were a man," Brugmann said. "But I suppose that is a luxury afforded gentlewomen."

"Your chauvinism is out of place here," Safiyya said. "The Ottoman Empire has quickly become a shining beacon of equality for women in the modern world."

"A proud boast for a land where the women must go veiled in public."

Safiyya pointed towards her face. "Do you see a veil, Mr. Brugmann?"

"What about... about harems?" Herbert said. "I'd heard that slavery for women was still common here."

She raised her fists to her shoulders. "Do you see shackles on my wrists? I was a slave in Macedonia for over half my life, even though the Sultan had declared it *yasadışı*. It was only when Cemal Bey and the Young Turks forced their reforms that I could walk free. Only after the coup could I attend university."

"Is it common for women here to seek higher education?" Aldora asked.

"The day the Young Turks mandated the colleges accept women the lines of those yearning to educate themselves stretched all along the *İstiklâl*

Caddesi as far as the eye could see. Women in the empire are becoming physicians, engineers, statesmen."

"A female engineer?" Brugmann said.

"The place of women in the Empire is stronger than anywhere in the world," Safiyya said. "I am proud to be a free woman of the Ottoman Empire."

"Amazing," Mme Viviani said.

"Quite." Aldora eyed the woman speculatively, a thousand questions on her lips.

"I do appreciate that even with our differences you have all made an effort to remain civil," Cemal said. "As a sign of my gratitude I would like to invite you all out for some entertainment on the morrow. We will set out for the *hamam* — a public bath — in the morning, take in some local theatre, and then finish up the evening with dinner at a Roma coffee house."

"I do enjoy a good steam," Herbert said.

"My husband and I trust you will understand if we do not attend?" Mme Viviani said. "We have business at the embassy."

"Unfortunate but understandable," Cemal said, bowing slightly. "Please tell me you at least will attend, Miss Fiske?"

The Englishwoman glanced reluctantly across the banquet room towards the table where her ward was dining with some of the less-important guests. Penny was idly picking at her food, chin propped up by an elbow on the table. "I would love to, but I promised my ward an outing into Stamboul..."

"The bathhouse is in Stamboul," Cemal said. "You and your ward can perhaps accompany us, and see to your outing afterwards?"

Aldora brightened. "In that case we would love to attend, Cemal Bey."

"Excellent!" Cemal spread his arms wide, as if to embrace the room. "Let me show you all the Constantinople that the Committee for Union and Progress has built. Take your experiences as a gift back to your people, and tell them that Europe's "Sick Old Man" has been revitalised with young blood!"

Penny had been petulantly disappointed with the delay in going to see her friend Kalil at first, initially refusing to disrobe for the bath, then refusing to stop pouting and leave the steam room, then stomping around the perimeters of the warm bath room in the wooden sandals the girls were given. When it became clear that nobody was paying much attention to her, she apparently forgot not to enjoy herself, and began drifting between the hot and cold pools, spending time immersed in both.

"I find it almost impossible to imagine living in a world where women are afforded the freedoms you say they have."

Aldora's eyes were half-lidded as she relaxed in the heat of the Turkish bath. She lay, nude, across a broad flat stone in the middle of a hot pool of water, one of the girl masseuses giving her a light massage, small fingers wrapped in rough gloves that exfoliated her skin even as they penetrated into the long lean muscles of her back. The steam-filled chamber was half-lit by stained windows set into its dome.

Safiyya laughed. "If you had told me just a few years ago that this is the way things were to be, I would not have believed it either."

Penny clopped back in from the cool chamber, drinking a spiced yogurt dessert.

"How did you get those scars?" she asked, pausing to stare openly at the female valet.

"Penelope!" Aldora gasped, half-rising from the stone's warmth, shocked into action by the girl's tactlessness.

"I do not mind her asking," Safiyya said. "The pain of my past is not something that shames me. Each mark is a reminder... of how far I have come, and of the good that Cemal Bey and the Committee have done for woman in the Empire."

She turned her back to the Englishwoman and her ward, allowing the woven cotton towel to slip from her shoulders to drape above her hips. Her back's chocolate-dark skin was marred with a series of old scars, raised and slightly lighter than her flesh, thin lines criss-crossing her back up to her shoulders. She pivoted, and Aldora saw that the scars crossed over her ribs along to her front, almost to her breast-bone. Similar scars crossed the tops of her thighs.

Her quiet words echoed loudly in the bath chamber. "I was taken from the Sudan as a child, when the Egyptian Army came to root out the remnants of the Mahdist rebels. They tore through our village, taking what they pleased, killing the men who didn't give them the answers they chose. They shot my father and took my mother, my sisters, and myself, and many of the other girls from the village."

"Why did they take you?" Penny asked.

"Slavery had been outlawed in the Empire the year I was born, but under Abdülhamid the ban was not much enforced in the outskirts of the Empire."

"You were a slave?"

"I remember a long march to the sea. I remember listening to the cries of the older women at night when the soldiers would... beat them... and worry if I was to be next. I remember a cramped boat that took me to a city

— İskenderiye, perhaps, or Suwais. A loathsome Macedonian merchant bought me and took me to his villa. He was an evil man, a cruel man, who took delight in harsh punishments for the smallest of slights."

"I'm so sorry for your pain," Aldora said.

"It is my pain that has made me strong," Safiyya said. "I survived. And when I was sixteen, I was rescued — saved by Cemal Bey. He killed the man who had been my tormentor, took me into his household, brought physicians to heal me. I owe him more than my freedom — I owe him my life."

"What an amazing story," Penny said.

"I am a learned woman, but for the time being I serve Cemal. Not because I am his, not because he owns me, not because I am woman and he man, but because I owe him a debt. It is not a debt I can ever repay, perhaps, but it is my choice to shoulder such obligation. In that, perhaps for the first time in my life, I have freedom."

The scars, Aldora decided, did not mar the dark woman's otherwise flawless skin. They were a sign of strength, a testament to what Safiyya could endure. She had little doubt that the woman's story was more traumatic and awful than the sanitised version she had told in front of Penny. To live as long as she had without hope of rescue, subjected to what amounted to torture and abuse... she could not say how she herself would fare under such treatment, or if she would not have simply taken her own life.

"You say you are educated?" Aldora said.

"I joined Cemal's household while he was an officer in Macedonia," Safiyya said, slipping her towel back over her shoulders, turning to dangle her powerful lean legs in the hot water. "I served him as *yaver* — what the English military would call a batman — even though I was not a soldier, and he taught me to read and write. After the revolution, and the colleges were made to admit women, Cemal Bey enrolled me in the law program at *İstanbul Darülfünûnu*."

"Law. Are you a solicitor?"

"I am trained in the law, and I volunteer to campaign for the rights of women in the Empire, but for now my chosen occupation is to serve Cemal Bey."

"Women seem to have so much more freedom here," Aldora said. "The transformation is amazing. I have to admit a degree of envy."

"If you're envious, then I'm doing my job as advocate well." Safiyya smiled.

Aldora chuckled, then sat up on the stone. "Where's Penny?"

"Your ward?" Safiyya turned to the bath attendant. "*Küçük kız nereye gitti?*"

FINE YOUNG TURKS

"*Çocuk sıcak bir odaya gitti*," the woman said.

"She's gone on to the next bath chamber."

Aldora sighed in frustration. "She's so impatient to go and see her friend."

"Let's go and fetch her," Safiyya said. "I will wait for the men in the coffee house, and you two can go meet this friend. I will pass your regards on to Cemal."

Aldora's felt her face colour. "Thank you, Safiyya."

The valet leaned forward conspiratorially. "He's rather fond of you, you know. I can tell."

"Well, I..." Aldora stammered. "I shall go and fetch Penelope, and we will meet you in the coffee house before we go."

Safiyya's mirthful laughter followed her as she slipped on her wooden sandals, grabbed her woven cotton towel, and quickly but stiffly walked from the room.

A long corridor led Aldora to the next chamber. Cemal Bey had reserved the baths for the early part of the day, and while he, Herr Brugmann, the Comte, and Mr. Herbert enjoyed the men's facilities, Aldora, Safiyya, and Penny had the women's half to themselves. Other than the attendant she'd left in the hot room with the valet she had not seen any staff; they must have been given the day off.

The facility's layout was similar to the Turkish baths popular in London. The first room had been dry but very hot, allowing a patron to steam themselves into a fine sweat. The second room, where she had left Safiyya, was serviced by warm water, where the bathers could cleanse themselves and relax. The third chamber was fed by a cool running stream, and had within it a number of small private relaxation nooks. She didn't see her ward upon entering.

"Penelope?" Aldora called, passing from alcove to alcove.

The cool room — *frigidarium* to the Romans, lord knew what the Turks called it — was the last stop before leaving, and the girls' clothing had been left — cleaned and neatly folded — in the niches. She found her own garments quickly enough, noted Safiyya's in the next niche, but Penny's were nowhere to be found.

Had the girl dressed and run off? Should she, Aldora, go after her, not knowing the city, or where this Kalil lived? Penny's father had let his daughter run freely through the great cities of Europe, but Aldora didn't feel comfortable not knowing where her adopted daughter was. Still, if Penny could take care of herself — and Aldora had no reason to believe otherwise — that left her free to stay with Cemal for coffee and the theatre afterwards...

Aldora's ruminations were interrupted when strong hands grabbed her from behind, heavy masculine arms wrapping around her torso, a solid forearm across her neck and one across her ribs. She was yanked back, off of her feet, only able to give the tiniest of yelps before the pressure at her throat cut the air from her lungs.

She struck back almost instinctively with her elbow, but her attacker was arched away, maintaining his grip while keeping himself out of range. She stamped back with the heel of her sandalled foot towards where she imagined his instep to be, but only managed to chip the bathhouse tiles.

Her vision began to grey out at the edges and the man pulled back on her neck again, almost bending her over backwards. She used that momentum to kick herself up and out of her sandals, feet scrabbling for purchase on the bathhouse wall, and launching herself into an almost vertical lift above her attacker. The sudden movement unbalanced him and sent him stumbling back into the cool water of the chamber's pool, letting go of the Englishwoman as he hit its surface.

Aldora pushed away from his body and turned to face the man who had grabbed her. He was a Turk; dressed in dark clothing, a curved dagger at his sash, floating motionless in the water. His head lay upon the edge of the pool where he'd fallen, his neck twisted at an unnatural angle where he'd landed on the edge. The assassin — if assassin he was — was dead.

Sudden fear for her ward's safety filled Aldora's mind. She pulled the dagger from the dead man's sash, climbed out of the pool, and ran back down the corridor to the warm room, bare feet slapping on the stone tile floor.

The warm room was empty, devoid of Safiyya or the bath attendant, so Aldora continued through it towards the steam room. There, she could see two figures partially concealed by the steam. The smaller one was undoubtedly the Sudanese woman, but the other figure — bulky, dressed in dark clothing, but with pale skin — was another assassin, and it looked as though he was creeping up on her friend.

Aldora's tread shifted to the balls of her feet, minimising the sound of her pace.

She practically flew into the hot steam room, launching herself at the assassin and driving her knee into the man's spine at the small of his back.

He buckled with a whining gasp. She grabbed the back of his head below the nape of the turban that he wore, using the force of her impact to drive the man crashing to the floor.

Safiyya whirled and gave a surprised cry at the sight of the unexpected melee.

The man rolled to the side, trying to throw Aldora off of his back as he drew his dagger. The Englishwoman was quicker and drew her own blade's curved edge across his throat, slicing open his trachea and ending his life with a helpless gurgle.

Safiyya stared down at the dead man with a mixture of horror and confusion on her face.

"Assassins!" Aldora said. "Another attacked me in the cool room."

Safiyya continued staring at her in shock for a moment before understanding broke over her face. "We must alert Cemal Bey!"

"Penny is missing," Aldora said. "We have to find her."

Safiyya ran towards the cold room, followed swiftly by her companion. "She may have escaped... you said yourself she was trying to sneak out. Running off after her into the city will only expose you to what killers remain."

Every instinct urged Aldora to go looking for her adoptive daughter, but the Sudanese woman was right. Cemal's resources were extensive, he knew the city, and he might have insight into who had tried to have her killed.

A stray thought almost stopped her cold, causing her to stumble. She had assumed the assassins were targeting her. It seemed she had the nasty habit of making enemies of dangerous men — but she'd been in the country for less than twenty-four hours, and hadn't given anyone cause to attack her. The fact that Safiyya had been attacked as well indicated that whatever was going on might not be about her.

She realised that, for once, she had no idea what was going on.

"What in blazes is going on?" the British ambassador asked.

"I wish I could tell you, Sir Lowther," Aldora said.

"The facts of the matter are quite plain," Cemal said, resting a bandaged hand on top of the conference table. His gaze passed from the Sir Lowther to the German, American, and French ambassadors, each of whom had gathered in the British embassy's conference room, along with the Bey, his guard captain Uğur, and Aldora.

"A gang of armed thugs covertly entered the hamam, bribing the staff to depart, and forcibly abducted Mr. Brugmann, Comte Montagni and Mr. Herbert, and attempted to abduct Ms. Fiske. They attempted to kill myself and my valet."

"I am unsurprised Ms. Fiske managed to fight them off," Sir Lowther said. "Formidable woman that she is."

Aldora managed not to grimace at the man, her face stone. She had little love for the overbearing knight.

"This is unacceptable," Von Bieberstein, the German Ambassador, said. "What are you doing to recover Herr Brugmann?"

Captain Uğur shifted uncomfortably in his seat. He was a large man — not fat, simply big, tall and broad. The elegantly carved wooden chair he sat in was insufficient to accommodate the width of his hips, and from the ginger way he shifted she believed that he feared a collapse at any moment.

"My valet is working with the police to find out whatever we can about these kidnappers," Cemal said. "I can assure you that the Committee of Union and Progress is making this a matter of highest priority."

"Do you believe Minister Viviani and his wife are to be targeted as well?" the French ambassador Bompard asked. Of those present, he was the eldest, his neatly trimmed beard and moustache a pure white. "They never arrived for their appointment."

"We fear so," Uğur said, his voice a low rumble, his English imprecise. "Men out looking for them, but for now we think they taken."

"So a coordinated attack?" American ambassador Rockhill asked. "What is it these assassins are after?"

"That has yet to be determined," Cemal said. "But rest assured, I will personally be investigating the matter."

Von Bieberstein folded his hands. "And you may 'rest assured', Cemal Bey, that the German Empire does not look kindly upon states that cannot guarantee the safety of its citizens."

"Nor does France," Bompard said. "Viviani is a government minister, for the love of God. I cannot guarantee that the Republic can leave this matter in the hands of the Ottoman Empire."

"I understand your positions," Cemal said, "and the Empire is grateful for any assistance the powers of Europe care to render. But understand, this is a matter of honour. It is only two years since the Committee took control, and foreign intervention would be seen by the monarchists as a sign of weakness, of letting Europe dictate Imperial policy. I trust I am not being too bold in saying that none of us — not the Young Turks, not your nations — want an Ottoman return to dictatorship."

"I understand the political implications," Bompard said, "But the decision is not mine to make."

"If France intervenes, so shall Germany." Von Bieberstein made a fist.

"I am not asking for a promise of non-intervention," Cemal said. "All I am asking for is time to uncover the conspiracy which has taken your citizens. Time to rescue them. Let us view this as an opportunity to forge stronger bonds between our peoples."

"I can support that," Rockhill said.

Ambassador Bompard drummed his fingers on the table. "I will do what I can to afford you the time you require."

"Such is all I ask."

"But you must keep the French embassy informed."

"Of course."

"And the German embassy," Von Bieberstein said.

"I will keep you all abreast of the progress of our investigation," Cemal said.

"Then Germany is satisfied," Von Bieberstein said. "For the time being."

Sir Lowther turned towards Aldora. "Oh, Miss Fiske. I am sorry you were exposed to this nasty business. I can arrange passage back to London immediately."

"I have no plans to leave Constantinople, Sir."

"I am afraid I must insist. Whatever the villain's nefarious plan is, the United Kingdom has been fortunate to have had its citizen escape it. Should you remain, the scoundrels will surely attempt to capture you again."

"I simply cannot depart, Sir Lowther. My ward is still out in the city, either on her own or captured by these men. I simply could not live with not doing all I could to recover her safely."

"This is highly irregular, Miss Fiske. It would be remiss of me to allow you to continue to endanger yourself."

"It is an irregular situation, and I am afraid I simply must insist." Aldora's tone remained as steady as her gaze, locked on to the Ambassador in a way which made it clear she would brook no argument.

The ambassador reddened, caught between two unacceptable choices.

Cemal held up a hand. "I may have a solution, Ambassador. What if Miss Fiske were to remain as a guest of my household, assisting in the investigation of this matter while continuing to search for her ward?"

"I would find it acceptable," Aldora said.

"I don't believe it entirely proper," Sir Lowther said. "Unmarried men and women should not cohabit, even in the short term. And Miss Fiske is a civilian—"

"A resourceful civilian, and one of the few witnesses to the kidnapper's assault," Cemal said.

"I am in favour of this course," Von Bieberstein said. "The conspirators may launch another attempt to take her and draw England into their plan."

"Are you seriously suggesting Miss Fiske be exposed to lure the villains into making another attempt at her capture?" Sir Lowther asked.

"She has not displayed any lack of bravery."

"She is a woman!"

"I'm willing to take the risk." Aldora shot a dirty look towards Sir Lowther. "Though I appreciate your concern."

"Unacceptable," the knight ground his teeth. "Your father shall hear of this."

Aldora's eyes narrowed.

He turned towards Cemal. "Surely, sir, you cannot permit the gentlewoman to put herself in harm's way?"

"I have found Miss Fiske to be a singularly capable woman," Cemal said. "In the new Ottoman Empire, women are trusted to make choices for themselves. She is an adult, and I will not — cannot — treat her like a child. If she so wishes to remain and seek her ward, then I will do whatever is within my power to ensure her safety while she does so. Not because she is a woman, but because she is a guest — of my country, and of my household."

Aldora had slowly turned to regard the Turk as he spoke, her face colouring slightly. While others had displayed confidence in her capabilities in the past, none had advocated for her quite so publicly. The reputation she held as a force to be reckoned with in London was unofficial, usually cushioned in the socially mandated hemming and hawing about her womanhood.

Cemal praised her, not as an exceptional woman, but as an exceptional person. That mattered most of all.

"I cannot argue the point with you, and I certainly cannot with her," Sir Lowther said. "She is the daughter of a very important gentleman — if you insist she stay over my objections, then I have no choice than to warn you that should she come to harm that the United Kingdom will not stand aside and give you the latitude of investigating."

"I understand, Sir Lowther."

"What you do not understand, my friend, is the lengths her father would go to should anything happen to her. My response will be through official channels. His will not."

Cemal glanced at the woman next to him and Aldora found she could not meet his gaze. "So be it, Ambassador."

Aldora and Cemal returned to the carriage awaiting them, the footman opening the door as they approached.

"I cannot abide that man." Aldora climbed into the carriage.

"Sir Lowther?" Cemal sat opposite her. "He is somewhat abrasive."

"I have known him for years," Aldora said. "Beginning when he served as Ambassador to Budapest and Tangier. I could not stand him then, and I cannot stand him now."

"Some in the Committee would share your view. The texts he's been publishing have been stirring up anti-Semitic sentiment among the Arab population."

"He's an instigator. Be careful, Cemal, or you will have the United Kingdom interfering in your business."

"If he will involve himself, he will. There's nothing I can do about it."

Aldora turned from the window as the carriage started moving. "Thank you for believing in me."

The Turkish gentleman clasped her hand in his own, and she felt her breath catch in her throat. "You should not thank me for having faith in you, Miss Fiske. You should trust that I respect you enough to acknowledge your capabilities."

"Cemal—" Aldora once again found speech difficult. "I cannot convey how much your faith means to me."

"Respect, real respect, should be so common in your life that it passes by unnoticed. I find it almost criminal the men of Europe do not recognise true strength. I meant it when I said that I would protect you, Miss Fiske, but not because I think you are in need of protection."

Her head swam. "Please. Call me Aldora."

Safiyya greeted the carriage when they arrived.

"The slain men carried no identification with them." She helped Aldora step down from the carriage, and then Cemal. "And the *hamam's* servants insist they were given no names. Police are circulating sketches of the dead men to try and find someone who recognises them."

"There is not much more to be done at the moment," Cemal said. "Safiyya, I want you to take Miss Fiske into Stamboul to look for her ward and this Kalil."

"I'm afraid all I really know of the boy is his name," Aldora said.

"No matter," Cemal said. "A young English girl on her own in Stamboul will not go unnoticed."

"Penelope does have a way of sticking out. Thank you, Cemal Bey."

"I will have a room made up for your return," Cemal said. "My private security is made up of men I with whom I served in the navy. They can be trusted."

"I feel safer already."

Cemal smiled. "Good luck with your search. Be safe, Aldora."

"I will. Thank you, Cemal."

The Turkish officer turned and strode into his palace, leaving the two women by the carriage.

Safiyya turned slowly to the English woman and grinned broadly. "You are utterly smitten."

"What? I am not!"

"No, you are. I do not intend to press a vein, but it is clear — the way you look at him, the way you speak. You are absolutely enamoured of Cemal."

Aldora's stomach dropped. "You don't hate me, do you? I know he's special to you."

Safiyya laid a hand on the Englishwoman's arm. "You overestimate our relationship. We are not lovers. We are friends of the soul. He saved me — gave me a life I never imagined I'd be able to live. He has my loyalty and my respect, but we are far too different for romance. Do not think I do not love Cemal. I do. But I love him as if he were an older brother."

Aldora nodded.

"You should be free to pursue a relationship with him. From what I have seen, you fit length to length, temperament to temperament. An exceptional match! And I know he likes you, too."

"The way I feel about Cemal... I haven't felt about anyone in a long time. But in a life here I would be giving up much... I don't know if I can turn my back on England. On my obligations."

Safiyya opened the carriage door. "It sounds to me like you're making more complications than there are. Cemal Bey changed my life for the better. I am sure if you gave him a chance he would do the same for you."

Aldora climbed in after her. She had a lot to think about.

Aldora and Safiyya spent hours fruitlessly searching the streets of Stamboul, looking for rumours of a young English girl with fire-red hair. None claimed to have seen her, and the few young boys named Kalil they ran across didn't know any Pennys, either. Aldora found herself moving through the foreign streets with a sense of heightened awareness, alert for any rough-looking men in dark outfits, on the look-out for potential ambushes. She knew another attack was imminent. She just didn't know when.

As the sky darkened the girls had little recourse but to return to Cemal's palace. Aldora tried to console herself with the notion that Penelope was a resourceful girl, used to spending weeks at a time alone in foreign cities, and well-acquainted with Constantinople. The girl would probably evade notice and pursuit better than Aldora herself would have been able to were their situations reversed.

Safiyya claimed a sudden but fierce headache upon returning, leaving Aldora to supper alone with Cemal. She did not complain.

With just the two of them dining, Cemal arranged for a smaller table to be brought out between them. A large loaf of round braided bread, sweet and rich to the palate, sat as centrepiece, and Aldora found herself served a plate of shredded lamb topped with tomato, cucumber, onion and a savoury white sauce. Thick frothy yogurt drinks served in large glass mugs.

"No rakı?" She smiled demurely.

"If you'd rather—"

"No, I don't mind. The rakı was a bit strong for me. I'm afraid I'm not much a drinker."

"There's a reason it's called lion's milk." He reclined on his pillows, leg bent, arm propping up his head.

"Is it? That's very funny."

He gestured towards her mug with his own. "This is *aryan*. It's quite good."

Aldora took a sip, then nodded. "Very tasty."

"Some make the claim that it dates all the way back to ancient Persia."

Aldora nodded, her eyes flickering to the door, to the window, to her hands.

"You're worried about your ward," Cemal said. "Forgive the inanity of my small talk."

"No, no. It helps. Distracts me. I'm not very used to... to doing nothing when something needs to be done."

"You're a strong woman, Miss Fiske."

"Please, call me Aldora."

Cemal chuckled. "I will try to remember. The Ambassador made such a fuss over your family name. The Fiskes."

"The Fiskes. Yes. A name that follows wherever I go."

"You do not get along with your father, I take it?"

"We're very different people," Aldora said. It wasn't a matter she liked to dwell upon, let alone speak of.

"As I was with my own father, a prominent mullah. We did not always see eye to eye. While tolerant of failings in others, he was always strict with me. I do suppose he is to thank for the opportunity to join the Young Turks — he was a Young Ottoman back in his own prime, and it was that connection that led the Turks to seek out my aid in the Rebellion."

"That was fortunate."

"I owe him much that I wish I did not."

Aldora picked at her plate. "My father. Lucian Calvin Fiske. Scion of one of the oldest noble houses in England. A popular saying goes that all you need to know of English gentry you can see in the eyes of a Fiske, and in a sense it's true. Father used to say we were what the other families aspired to be. I was raised to be the ideal others fell short of."

"That must have been a heavy burden to bear."

"Perhaps?" Aldora looked towards the balcony. "I knew no other way, growing up. Regiment. Discipline. The tyranny of tea-time. My brother used to say that if you cut a Fiske, we bleed Union Jack. We are not English, we are the English."

She trailed off. "He's dead now."

"Your brother?"

"I killed him." She rose and stepped away from the table, towards the balcony overlooking Constantinople's bay.

Cemal did not respond, just watching her move through the shadows.

"I killed my brother, the only one in my family whom I truly loved. We were all one another had, you understand, in the days of our youth. We had that bond, growing up Fiske. Raised to love queen and country, but most of all family, and he saw through it all long before I ever did. He saw the dark spots in our family portraits, the ones behind our parents' eyes. Even after they sent him away, after he went to study in Paris, we kept in touch. His correspondence allowed me to go on with the masquerade of being a gentlewoman while at home. And then I killed him."

Cemal rose, crossing the dining room to join her near the balcony. "Why?"

"Because he was sick," Aldora said. "Suffering an illness of the spirit. At first I thought it something he'd picked up in Paris, a disease of the mind. I won't lie, it's what I wanted to believe, somehow my poor sweet brother Grayson had been seduced by criminal anarchists into their twisted philosophies. After his death I realised he had let himself become cruel and callous because of our family, because of our parents."

"You speak of it like a mercy killing." Cemal's voice was gentle, his tone soft.

"Mercys, in a way, but pity wasn't why I had to kill him. He hurt many people. I... as much as I loved my brother, as a Fiske I have a responsibility, a noblesse oblige, burned into my soul. In killing Grayson I would suffer, but it was what was Right. What must have been done for the greater good of the English people."

"I understand, perhaps more than you know," Cemal said. "I betrayed my military vows when I joined the Young Turks in their coup, but I did what I thought best for the Turkish people. And for all the peoples of the Empire."

"My fiancé said he understood. Does it shock you? To hear I am an engaged woman? Carrying on with you as I do?"

"No."

"He claimed to understand, but I don't think he could. He's never had to make that sort of choice. I think, though... I think you understand."

Cemal stood close behind Aldora, his arms wrapping around her front, his hot breath on the back of her neck. "I do."

She leaned back into him, into his embrace, into his body. It would be so easy to let go, to forget about her life in England, about her family, about Alton, about the responsibilities of being an Englishwoman. The need to lose herself in Cemal's arms, to lose herself in Constantinople, to give herself up to a man who saw her as a person first and a woman second, to a culture poised on the cusp of recognising the universal rights to which women were due... if only she could forget what it meant to be Fiske.

To be a Fiske meant to do right, even at the cost of your own happiness, simply because it was the more difficult path.

Maybe she'd had enough of it.

She felt Cemal pull away, and he took a piece of her soul with him, replacing it with longing.

"You've had a trying day, Aldora. Tomorrow we rise at Dawn, and I will lead a police unit into Stamboul, and we will continue our search for your ward."

She turned towards him, taking his hand in her own. "Aren't the great powers expecting you to focus on finding the kidnappers?"

"Right now your well-being is more compelling to me than their demands."

"Cemal..."

He reached up and cupped the side of her jaw in his palm. "You have a choice to make, Aldora. Perhaps the most important of your life. Of both our lives, and you will be unable to make it until you have your Penelope at your side. To me, that is more important than the anger of the European powers."

She closed her eyes, feeling a hot tear roll down her cheek. This was too much, Cemal's understanding, his touch, the way he looked at her... was all too big, too much, too fast. He was right. She needed rest. She needed a clear head.

She sniffled, opened her eyes, and nodded.

The guest room Cemal had provided her was sumptuous in the extreme, ornate embroidered furnishings centred around a broad canopied bed, its mattress as soft as a cloud. A shuttered balcony looked out over the Bosporus Strait, wine dark waters bisecting the city, the pilot lights of airships crossing far above. It would have been beautiful if she had not been so exhausted.

Her back hit the bed and she kept falling, sinking, descending into the warm close oblivion of sleep, too tired even to dream of olive skinned men with eyes of deep hazel.

Instinct dies hard and Aldora slipped out of bed before she even realized the bells had woken her. Masculine shouts of alarm came from the hall. She grabbed a translucent shawl from one of the bed-posts to wrap around her shoulders before striking out into the corridor.

A pair of guards ran past, one with a torch, the other a rifle. Aldora slipped into the hallway and followed them, shawl held close at her neck.

They lead her to a larger group of guards, some with rifles, some pistols, some torches, all talking in Turkish. Safiyya, hastily dressed in her valet's skirt and jacket, was coordinating their actions.

"What's going on?" Aldora asked.

"Someone tried to break into the palace," Safiyya said. "Go back to your room — the halls aren't safe."

"Is it any safer in my quarters?"

"No, but I'll feel better if I know where you are," Cemal said, hastening to join the group.

"*Üç - sol koridora gidin*," Safiyya said to half of the men, and then continued to the others, "*Geri kalanlar mutfakta kontrol edin.*"

The men departed, weapons and light sources in hand.

"It must be the kidnappers, trying to abduct you from beneath my very nose." Cemal pounded his fist into his palm.

"Perhaps you should return to the embassy," Safiyya said. "If they would strike here—"

"I will not be chased away," Aldora said. "Not without my ward, and not under anyone else's terms."

"You're far braver than most," Cemal said, fingers lightly touching her hand. "But if you are to remain, I must insist that you stay within these walls."

She turned her wrist, clasping his arm briefly. "But Penelope—"

He took her aside by the arm, speaking softly. "I insist. I can help protect you, here, while searching for the girl in the city. I cannot search for her if I have to worry about you, too."

Aldora dropped her eyes. "I don't think any place is safe."

"None will be. Not until we discover who is after you, and why. Until then... until then we must be very careful."

She nodded and reluctantly let go of his hand.

"Return to your room." Cemal said. "Get some rest."

"I'll try."

FINE YOUNG TURKS

The next day Aldora joined Safiyya and the palace staff in the dining hall for a breakfast of fried spicy dry sausage, eggs, and sweet black tea. Cemal and several of his guards had departed in the early morning to search the old city for Penelope or signs of the kidnappers, and while Aldora couldn't understand their chatter, the attitude among the servants was one of nervous anticipation. Safiyya looked more excited than worried, though, and she kept pumping Aldora for information about her dealings with Cemal.

"A lady does not discuss such things."

"She doesn't?" Safiyya said. "What's the point of having exploits, if not to share them with your girlfriends?"

"A lady does not have exploits."

"I don't think I'd much enjoy being one of your ladies."

Aldora allowed herself a small smile. "Penelope has said the same thing, on multiple occasions."

"Your bond with your adoptive daughter is strong, isn't it?"

"I'd like to think so," Aldora said. "I'm all she has."

"Being an orphan is difficult," Safiyya said. "No matter the circumstance."

"I have always been of the opinion that the family you create for yourself is more important than the family you are born into," Aldora said.

"That's not very English."

"Truth be told, many of my attitudes are not. I've struggled against what I was raised to be and who I really am for most of my life."

"It's sounds as if you tire of leading a double life."

Aldora looked down at her plate, mopping up the grease from her eggs with a crust of bread. "I think I very much am. In London all eyes are upon me, watching for the opportunity to gossip or to put a Fiske in her place."

Safiyya made a sour face. "Gossips and wags."

"They're why I travel. The further from London I roam, the fewer expectations are placed upon me, the more... genuine I can be."

"Constantinople and Cemal are far from London, Aldora."

The Englishwoman made a face. "I, while remaining prim and proper when the eyes of society are upon me..."

"...would much rather be a free woman."

"Yes."

"Like the women, here, in Constantinople."

"...yes."

"Then is your course not clear?"

Aldora didn't respond. Safiyya had come from a truly horrible situation. It was no great tragedy to leave behind a legacy of slavery and abuse. But Aldora had had her English mindset drilled into her from a young age, raised to be a Gentlewoman, to be Fiske. The lessons she'd learnt had hooks sunk deep into her psyche, and extracting them wasn't a simple matter of picking up and moving.

No matter how badly she might want to.

The waiting was not easy. As beautiful and expansive as Cemal's palace was, Aldora was not used to being cooped up inside all day long. Back in London she'd scheduled her days full of the obligations that befell a woman of her stature; social calls, shopping, games of lawn tennis or croquet, rural horseback rides. Here, corridor after corridor of gilt mosaic offered no distraction from her worries about her adopted daughter, and even the expansive library held no escape, for she could read no Turkish or Arabic. With Safiyya gone to run errands in the afternoon, she found herself aimless, adrift, and feeling a little alone.

Like it was when she was a girl.

Could she do it? Leave London behind? Leave the world as she knew it, turn her back on everyone she knew, for a small chance of happiness in Cemal's arms? It wasn't the responsible thing. It wasn't the logical thing. But it was what she wanted.

Wasn't it enough?

Cemal hadn't returned by the time Aldora retired for the evening, and this time her dreams were troubled, fitful. Again and again she revisited the same scenarios; her lonesome upbringing in her parents' Yorkshire estate as a small girl alone in a big empty house, the social manoeuvring of the London season, striking an agreement with her fiancé. She woke several times, tossing and turning, worried about Penny, the turmoil she felt over the choice between returning to London to marry Alton, and giving it all up to remain in Constantinople with Cemal lay in her belly like a red hot bowl of molten disquiet.

She was awake in the early morning hours, staring through the gauze of the bed's canopy towards the ceiling, when the alarm bells rang again.

Another attempted kidnapping? So soon after the last?

Aldora lurched out of bed, grabbing her shawl, and ran out into the hall again. She could hear the sounds of conflict from elsewhere in the palace — clashing blades, masculine Turkish curses, and the pounding of the guards' boots as they converged on the intruder's location.

Safiyya stepped out of a cross-hall and grabbed her by the shoulders as she headed towards the commotion. "Wait! It isn't safe. Let the guards handle the intruder."

She struggled in the valet's strong grip. "Let me go! He might know where Penny is!"

"After his last attempt he's almost certainly armed," Safiyya said.

"I can handle a little swordplay!"

"I'm sure you can. But you're unarmed." Safiyya let the woman go, pulling a sabre from the wall, offering it to her hilt first.

The Englishwoman took it hesitantly. It was old, and with a sharper curve than the fencing weapons she was accustomed to, and it flared out wider in its furthest third. Still, the balance was good, and the steel seemed strong. She could handle it.

"I give you this for your protection, but Cemal's men have orders to take the intruder alive," Safiyya said. "He trusts them to keep us safe. You can trust them to do their jobs."

Somewhat mollified, Aldora nodded slightly. "Let's head in that general direction, though."

"Okay. But slowly. We don't want to get underfoot."

The fighting was over by the time Aldora and Safiyya arrived, and most of the guards had dispersed, save for a pair having minor scratches bandaged up. Cemal was talking to guard captain Uğur, but headed over when he saw the girls approach.

"Another intruder?" Safiyya asked.

"Yes," Cemal said. "This one we managed to take alive."

"Let me see him," Aldora took Cemal's hand. "I must know if they have Penelope."

Cemal brought her hand to his lips, brushing against her skin with the lightest of kisses. "You don't speak Turkish, my dove, and I've had my men deliver him to the French Embassy."

"To Ambassador Bompard?" Aldora asked. "But why?"

Cemal let her hand go. "The situation with the European Powers grows ever more tense. No one has heard from Minister Viviani or his wife since the initial attack, and Bompard has had little luck in persuading his government to let us handle matters. If the French intervene, the Germans will not be far behind."

"Is military intervention a possibility?"

"It is seeming more and more likely. I'm doing what I can to forestall it, but it is only a matter of time before the kidnappers make their demands."

"What could they possibly want?" Aldora asked.

"Concessions, possibly," Safiyya said. "Many in the empire are tired of European interference in the Balkans. They circle like vultures over the provinces they covet to expand their own colonial holdings."

"The great powers of Europe would never let a conspiracy of kidnappers dictate their foreign policy," Aldora said.

"Small concessions can have large effects down the road," Safiyya said. "But who can say what the kidnappers believe?"

"It's late," Cemal said. "I've a long day of placating the French tomorrow, and I'd rather be present for the interrogation."

"May I attend as well?"

Cemal and Safiyya exchanged a glance.

"It would be safer if you stayed within the palace," Cemal said. "At least for now."

"I can handle—"

"I am well aware that you can handle yourself, brave one, but I cannot handle the thought of you endangering yourself needlessly," Cemal held Aldora by the forearms. "I need my wits about me when I deal with Bompard tomorrow. Please, stay in the palace."

"Very well," Aldora leaned against Cemal, her cheek against his chest. "But tell me everything he says upon your return."

"That I shall. Now go to bed."

"Yes, darling."

The next day found Aldora confined to her room.

Uğur, assigned to guard her door, was apologetic with what little English he spoke. "Many sorries. Cemal Bey say much intruders in palace. Keep *Khanum* safe in room."

"This is intolerable!" Aldora slapped the frame of the door. "I demand you let me out at once."

"*Üzgünüm*. Sorry. Sorry."

"Then I demand you fetch Safiyya immediately!"

His brow furrowed, and he spoke with hesitance. "*Birçok affeder*, many pardons, but *uşak* Safiyya is with the Bey."

Aldora slammed the door in the big man's face, fuming that Cemal would restrict her in such a fashion. It wasn't Uğur's fault, the guard was simply obeying his master, but she was not content to be locked away like some mewling child. That was one thing that Cemal would have to learn if she were to stay in Constantinople with him: Aldora Fiske was no helpless girl to be coddled and protected. She dressed hurriedly, angrily.

She marched over past her bed and threw open the shutters to the balcony and peered over the edge. It was a sheer drop down a jagged cliff to sharp rocks and the Bosporus below — there was no way she could scale it, and even if she did she'd only end up in the strait's cold waters. She tilted her head, looking upwards, and saw that strong ivy wove up a trellis along the wall to the balcony above. She tied her boots' together by the laces and slung them around her neck, her bare toes having better purchase for climbing. Without further hesitation she pulled herself over and on to the trellis.

Inch by inch she ascended, the wooden lattice groaning under her slight weight, careful not to put too much pressure on any parts not supported by strong ivy, careful not to risk dizziness by looking into the churning waters below. In mere minutes she had reached the upper balcony, climbed over it, and discovered herself to be in what looked like a study. Row upon row of books filled shelves lining the walls alongside scroll-racks. A heavy smell of incense filled the air, faint smoke wafting from an extinguished stick sitting atop a writing desk near the door.

Aldora quickly donned her boots, then crept over to the door, only to find it secured by a large and antique looking ward lock.

She headed over to the desk, in search of a key. The drawers proved full of paper, ink stones, and calligraphy nibs, but her eyes were drawn to the letter secured by callipers on top of the desk. To her surprise, it was written in English.

> *Dear Gentlemen,*
>
> *It is with great regret that I must inform you that my investigations have turned up evidence that the driving force behind the kidnapping of your countrymen is none other than a faction within my own Committee of Union and Progress. Misguided elements which no doubt seek to gain leverage over your activities within the Ottoman sphere have no doubt taken it upon themselves to hold your citizens for ransom. These tactics are not the agenda of the Young Turk movement, and we officially disavow such underhanded tactics.*
>
> *I, Cemal Yavuzade Bey, offer both my sincere apologies and renew my dedication to ferreting out the subversive elements within the Committee for the good of Europe and Ottoman alike. The CUP cannot deny culpability in letting these rogue elements sully our good name, and it is vital for a young*

government to regain the good-will of its neighbours. On behalf of the Committee, I declare my willingness to consider any concessions you required in exchange for your continued good will, and only ask in return that, when the factions within the Ottoman government vie for control in the wake of this scandal, you remember it was Cemal Yavuzade Bey who displayed such willingness to work with foreign interests.

*Your humble servant,
Cemal Bey*

Aldora read the letter twice over, trying to glean its meaning. The obsequious tone didn't sound like the confident Cemal she knew... and a Young Turk faction was behind the kidnappings? He hadn't mentioned anything like this to her, and judging from the dryness of the ink it had to have been written at least a day prior.

This talk of concessions — it seemed to fly in the face of Safiyya's own views of appeasement. Was this some baroque political manoeuvring on Cemal's part, or did he actually intend to surrender to the European powers the provinces they hungered for?

The only way she'd find the truth would be to ask him. Aldora carefully removed the note from his writing desk and slipped it into her breast pocket, before returning to the window.

Gingerly she climbed back down to her own balcony, then opened the hall door a crack.

Uğur regarded her sternly.

"Can I have something to eat?" she asked. "Some breakfast?"

"Oh," he grinned pleasantly. "Yes. I have something sent?"

"Can't you just escort me to the kitchens?"

"No no. Is danger. Prisoner in *zindan* but still danger of more." He turned to go. "You wait. I get platter for breaks-fast."

She reached out and tugged on his sleeve. "Hold on. What did you say? Prisoner? Zindin?"

"*Zindan*. It being... place for criminal? Down below? Under palace?"

"Do you mean a dungeon?" Aldora asked. "The intruder from last night is here? In the palace?"

Uğur nodded. "Yes. But no worry. Is lock up in *zindan*. No troubles."

The guard ambled off toward the kitchens, leaving Aldora alone with her thoughts. Cemal had outright lied to her, had told her the intruder had been delivered to the French embassy. Why? To protect her? To make her feel safe? She would have been but slightly offended at his duplicity, but in the light of the letter she'd taken from his study — what did it all mean? There were too many missing pieces of the puzzle for her to glean a complete picture, but what she could make out did not paint Cemal in the best light.

What did she really know about him anyway?

Here she was, ready to throw her old life away, and why? Because of a few smoldering glances? A kind word? A handsome face? She was no blushing schoolgirl, ignorant of men and romance. She'd had lovers, more than proper to admit. She'd seen the world, seen other cultures beyond the confines of the city. A love-sick child was not who she was.

It was the promise of freedom which had called to her. While she appreciated Cemal's attention, Safiyya's words were what had seduced her. The story she told of an empire where women were free to marry or live single, one where they could raise children or have a career. She'd spent her life subverting the restrictions the English Way had placed upon her because of the fact that she had happened to have been born an upper class gentlewoman. The idea that, here, in Constantinople, she might not have to pretend was intensely alluring.

Answers. She needed answers. Cemal would return later, but she didn't have to wait until then.

Aldora stole off down the corridor opposite the way Uğur had gone, the sabre Safiyya had given her held in a reverse grip parallel to her arm. She'd been confined to the palace long enough to learn its corridors, and darted from shadow to shadow like a ghost, avoiding the gaze of guards and servants alike. A short jaunt took her to the palace's ground floor, and it didn't take much longer for her to find stairs heading into the depths below the palace.

Unlike the sumptuously appointed above-ground, the stairs leading to the zindan were starkly functional, with rough cut stone, slick with groundwater from the nearby strait. Aldora's footsteps echoed back up to her with every step, and an earthy musty smell filled her nostrils.

The basement was practically medieval in appearance, straw on the floor absorbing most of the salt-water the walls were sweating. Two pitch torches provided all that illumination in the long corridor running to the back of the palace, and she counted six cells on each side.

She walked between them, peering into their empty chambers through bars in the heavy wooden doors. They had little appointment, being closer to oubliettes for the forgotten than any humane cell. It disturbed her that her Cemal should have such a thing in his cellar.

The last cell was occupied by a man bound with thick leather straps to a sturdy wooden chair, his head bowed, his chest and feet bare. He looked up blearily as she opened the door to his cell, and Aldora all but recoiled at the sight of the man's face — bruised and beaten, almost unrecognisingly bloodied. His chest, too, showed the signs of torture, large darkening bruises and deeper red lash-marks. Aldora had killed men before, had beaten them in physical combat, but the sight of someone who had been abused, helpless, still managed to turn her stomach.

Barbaric.

"You poor wretch." She had intended to question him — harshly — but seeing what had been done to him just left her with a sense of unnerved pity. Was this the handiwork of the man she'd been enamoured of?

Moved by pity, she pulled over the cell's bucket of water and wrung out the sponge floating within, using it to clean the blood away from the man's eyes.

"Msss," he moaned.

She shushed him. "Rest now. You'll probably need it."

"Mish Fishke," he said.

She stopped, hand frozen. "You... you speak English?"

"'M English."

Aldora dropped the sponge.

He took a long breath. "Fah. Your father. Sent me."

"My... my father sent you?" Her face turned white in the torchlight.

"Sent me. Rescue you."

Aldora knelt before the man, tilting his head up, hand cupping some of the relatively clean water from the bucket to his lips. He drank greedily.

"Mr. Fiske sent me to recover you." His voice grew stronger, and he tried to focus on her face.

"Rescue me from what?"

"Went missing. Young girl — Penelope said."

"Penelope?" Aldora said. "You've seen her? Is she alright?"

"She's fine," the man said.

Aldora began working at the straps binding the man. "What's your name?"

"Rowe. Thomas... Thomas Rowe."

Aldora offered him some more water. "What happened to Penelope, Mr. Rowe?"

"She... she'd left the bath before the kidnapping, and spent the day with her friend in Stamboul. In the evening she attempted to covertly return to the palace, only to find it locked tight."

"She could have just come to the door," Aldora said. "She was probably worried I'd be cross."

"Be grateful she did," Rowe said. "She overheard the guards discussing the kidnapping as if they'd been involved. When they discovered her, she fled."

"The guards?" Aldora asked. "Which guards?"

"Listen ca-carefully, Miss Fiske. Penelope returned to the Embassy with what she'd heard. Lowther questioned Cemal Bey, who reasoned some of his guards must have been involved, and declared he'd investigate—"

"Cemal told me none of this."

"Listen. This... the important part. Said that you yourself had been kidnapped."

Aldora stopped unstrapping the man. "But... that makes no sense!"

Rowe maintained steady eye contact with the woman. "That's when Sir Lowther telegrammed your father with the news."

"Unless," Aldora felt faint. "Unless Cemal himself is involved in the kidnapping."

The straps binding his arms undone, Rowe helped Aldora with the ones binding his legs. "I arrived in Istanbul and began trying to hunt you down, on your father's orders. Rumour directed me to an Englishwoman kept in Cemal Bey's palace, and I attempted an infiltration."

Aldora remained silent.

He exhaled and tried flexing his arms. "They caught me, beat me, and have been torturing me down here."

"I've got to get you out of here," she said.

"Back to the embassy."

Aldora helped the man to his feet. "Can you walk?"

He wavered. "I can manage. With difficulty."

Rowe leaned on Aldora while the two left his cell. Betrayal and confusion warred within the gentlewoman's mind, Rowe's account filling in a few of the missing pieces in the puzzle of Cemal's letter. She was so lost in thought that she didn't spot Safiyya sneaking up on the pair of them until the valet attacked.

Aldora pushed Rowe out of the way and pivoted along the wall, leaving the Sudanese woman's chopping blade to spark against the stone where she'd been a moment before.

"I'm sorry to have to kill you, sister," Safiyya said.

"Safiyya, wait!" Aldora said. "This man isn't—"

"She knows," Rowe said. "She's the one that did this to me."

Aldora stared at the woman, horrified.

A cold light shone in the Safiyya's eyes. "It takes the tortured to know how to really hurt a man."

"How could you?"

Safiyya slashed out at Aldora again, and the gentlewoman managed to shake off her shock enough to bring her own blade to the fore, barely deflecting the vicious attack.

"Cemal saved me. I owe him my life, my freedom."

Aldora stood over the fallen Rowe, pivoting her grip on the sword from the reversed to a forward defensive grip, one hand on the hilt, the other flat against the flat edge of the tip. "So you would let him use you?"

"I let no man use me!" Safiyya snarled, feinting with a lunge, following up with a quick tip slash that almost took Aldora's eyes. "Never again. I agree with Cemal, with his plan. Our hostages give us leverage to keep Europe at bay and out of Asian affairs. They will give us a stronger Empire."

"You're wrong." Everything finally made sense, Aldora finally had an understanding of Cemal's plan. "Cemal is using you. He intends to betray the conspiracy to the European Powers in exchange for personal political favours. He's a traitor to you, and to the Empire!"

"You lie!" Safiyya shouted, swinging high. Aldora ducked below the attack, only to take the Sudanese valet's knee to her face.

She stumbled back, stunned, the sword dropping from her hand.

"I am sorry it had to end like this," Safiyya said. "Take solace in the fact that your sacrifice will result in betterment for the lot of women in the Empire."

"We were friends!"

"My cause is too important for friendship." The woman drew her sword back, ready to skewer Aldora.

"Wait!" Aldora said, drawing Cemal's letter from her pocket. "Before you strike, read this!"

Safiyya snatched the paper from Aldora's hand with a look of mixed pity and scorn.

"Do you honestly think I will be dissuaded by..." she trailed off as she read the first few lines.

"It's Cemal's handwriting. You know it to be so."

As she reached the end Safiyya staggered back and bent double, as if from a physical blow. "No."

"Safiyya..."

The girl looked up, pain and sorrow etched on her face. "This is a lie!"

"It is Cemal's handwriting, is it not?"

She looked back down at the letter. "He... I... Cemal started the Fellowship of Ottoman Strength. He recruited me... he recruited all of us! It was his cause!"

"He's using you, Safiyya! He set this entire affair up to bolster his own political agenda."

The valet balled the note up in her hand and spoke in a flat, dead voice.

FINE YOUNG TURKS

"Go. Take the prisoner and go. I will deal with Cemal when he returns."

"Where are the other kidnapped Europeans being kept?"

"Only Cemal knows."

"We need him alive, to tell us where they are."

"I will deal with Cemal. I will not let myself be used. Not by any man. Not even by Cemal."

Rowe pulled himself laboriously to his feet. "But the French, Germans, and Italians already have air-fleets on the way. They won't be satisfied without a culprit to stand trial."

"Just as Cemal had intended," Aldora said.

"I do not care!" Safiyya rounded on Aldora, sword held tightly in her hand. "You of all people understand how I have been betrayed. You know where I was — what I was before he rescued me. You know what I owe him. You know how he has used that to manipulate me."

"I know," Aldora said quietly. "Safiyya, I know. And I know all too well what it is to need to right a wrong. If you kill him, it is only vengeance."

"Vengeance is all I need!"

"But if we take this note to the Young Turk leadership, and it is Cemal who faces the Great Powers' wrath for this crime, if it is his own wretched plan that is his downfall... that is not only vengeance. That is divine justice."

"Cemal's personal ornithopter is kept on the roof," Safiyya said quietly. "We will take it to Dolmabahçe Palace, and I will turn myself over to the Committee authorities."

"You don't need to turn yourself in," Aldora said. "The letter and Rowe's testimony should be enough."

"No," Safiyya said. "It must be personal. Do you understand?"

"But they may call for your execution!"

"I know."

Aldora closed her eyes, blinking away exhausted tears. Safiyya helped her support the sagging Rowe, and the three made their way out of the dungeon.

They hadn't gone far before the alarm sounded.

"I can hold them off," Safiyya said, "while you escape with the note."

"I don't know how to fly an ornithopter."

"Then let us be swift."

The palace servants got out of the way as the three stumbled up the stairs and down the hall towards the palace roof. Cemal's ornithopter waited ready at the far end, a trio of guards keeping watch over it. Rowe leaned against the parapet while Aldora and Safiyya rushed to engage them.

The Englishwoman had adapted her fencing training to the curved blade quite adeptly, knocking one guard's blade aside with a clang before hooking around the second's calf and ripping through his hamstring with a back-slice. He fell screaming and clutching his ruined calf, while the first guard made a second attempt to cleave her skull.

Aldora pivoted to the side and drew the edge of her sword's blade diagonally across his chest, slicing through his shirt and vest and flaying him open.

She turned from him as he fell, in time to see Safiyya kicking the third guard from the roof, impaled by his own blade.

"That was... I don't know how to feel about that," Rowe said as the women returned for him.

"Grateful," Safiyya said.

"Quite. And a little intimidated."

"Good," Aldora said.

They helped Rowe into the back, and Safiyya climbed into the pilot's seat.

Aldora climbed in last, ending up leaning slightly out through 'thopter's open frame. "It's rather cramped."

"These are designed for one pilot and one passenger at best."

"Can it get off the ground with the three of us?"

"It will have to. But don't worry. I have strong legs, and the anger fuelling them burns like the sun." A look of fierce determination crossed Safiyya's face and she drew back her skirt, exposing her long muscular calves as she slid her feet into the machine's pedals. She grit her teeth and began peddling, the vehicles mechanical articulated wings slowly beginning to flap. She peddled harder and harder, and the craft began to rise from the roof.

"Can you manage?" Aldora asked.

"It gets easier when we're moving."

The ornithopter rose unsteadily into the sky, dipping off of the roof but not losing too much altitude. Aldora stared at the sky ahead as they circled back towards the Bosporus. If Safiyya's strength flagged, if the strain of the three passengers was too much for the machine, it would go crashing into the swift waters below.

"We have company," Rowe said.

Aldora looked back. Three more craft rose from the palace grounds.

"More ornithopters," she said. "And they're catching up to us!"

"The guards' craft," Safiyya said. "With our weight, there's no way we can outrun them. And they're armed."

"Here," Rowe pulled a rifle out of the back, handing it to the gentlewoman. "You know how to use this?"

"Of course," Aldora said. "It's an Enfield."

"Then use it."

Aldora leaned sideways out of the craft's frame, tilting it alarmingly. "Sorry."

"Just shoot them!"

She took a careful aim at the closest vessel, eventually settling on the pilot as a target of opportunity. The crack of the rifle was deafening in the small space, and Aldora was rewarded by the sight of the ornithopter's wings drooping. Moments later it fell from the sky like a stone, and she pulled the rifle's bolt back, chambering the next round. The chamber and magazine had been altered for a smaller round than the Enfields she was used to, but it was sufficient for the task at hand.

She shifted slightly, hanging a bit further out, knees hooked around the 'thopter's side rail.

From this vantage she could see that the guards' vehicles had a gatling mount on their undersides, and the closest one's chamber had begun to spin. Knowing that the heavy-duty rounds would tear through their own vessel like tissue paper, she willed herself calm, took careful aim at where she gauged the gun's magazine to be, tightened her grip, and fired.

The resulting explosion's shock-wave rocked the ornithopter and she would have fallen from it had Safiyya not reached out and steadied her leg.

"Thank you," she said, heaving herself back in and pulling back on the rifle's bolt. The third vehicle veered off, returning towards Cemal's estate.

"No stomach for it, that one," Rowe said.

Aldora declined to comment, handing the rifle back to him.

The public uproar over what became known as "the Yavuzade Letter" was riotous. The European powers demanded a full investigation and return of their citizenry. Most of the Young Turk leadership agreed, but a significant portion — mostly Turkish nationalists — chose to side with Cemal Bey, airship captain hero of the revolution, when he feigned ignorance of what he called slander. A trial was held, with much evidence provided for the consumption of the public in Istanbul and abroad, but the real decisions were made in small rooms by men empowered in such matters by their own governments.

It went on for weeks, and while she was not privy to the true negotiations, Aldora stayed in the British Embassy and repeatedly refused offers of passage home. Safiyya had been taken into custody upon turning herself over to authorities, and the Englishwoman was determined to see things out, for her friend's sake if nothing else. Beyond being asked for a written statement, Aldora was left to her own devices, her good name kept out of the official records.

On the fifth day members of the city police just so happened to find the kidnapped foreigners, alive and unharmed but unaware of the mastermind behind the plot, and Aldora knew that some deal had been brokered with Cemal.

The Bey himself was free to come and go on his own recognisance. Despite the allegations, the Turkish papers were careful to clarify that he was working with the investigation to clear his name.

She spoke to him only once, boldly slipping into his carriage when it had stopped at an intersection.

"Why?" was all she asked.

Cemal had levelled his gaze at her, betraying no surprise over her sudden appearance, no guilt or shame in his eyes. "Why?"

"You led me on. You used me. You used Safiyya. You owe me an explanation."

"The days of empires are behind us, Miss Fiske. The world isn't small enough to accommodate them. Change is in the air, and its name is Nationalism. A large multi-ethnic Ottoman cannot long stand, but with my actions... we will see a strong Turkey emerge from its ashes."

"That's not what I asked."

"Why you?"

"Why me."

"You were a means to an end. It was nothing personal."

Her voice was utter calm. "Nothing personal."

"No."

It took all her willpower not to spit in the man's face. She slipped out of his carriage, and into the city.

On the final day of the trial Aldora donned her coat, laced up her boots, wore her best hat, grabbed her parasol, and chartered a carriage to take her to the courthouse. In the Embassy lobby she was met by a slightly built older gentleman — perhaps sixty — with carefully groomed hair, a trimmed Van Dyke beard, and an exquisitely tailored suit.

"Hello, father," she said.

"Aldora." His tone was outwardly pleasant.

"I was on my way to the courthouse." Her voice did not falter. "Did you come all the way across the world to escort me?"

FINE YOUNG TURKS

"Why do you bother? You know how this all ends."

"How, perhaps. What I don't know is why."

"Yes you do." He leaned sideways against the door-frame. "The powers of Europe get another claim on the Balkans. The Empire is spared the indignity of one of its heroes being exposed a monster. Condemned criminals will be blamed, and the people's need for closure will be satiated by their blood. It's the same as it ever was."

"And Safiyya? She was just a tool in this. Will she be vindicated as well, or is she another sheep upon the altar of public blood-lust?"

Her father made a sour face. "Come, Aldora. Young Penelope is waiting for you back in England, as is your gentleman fiancé."

"It isn't enough."

"You feel wronged, I know. You want revenge?"

"I want justice."

"Justice." Her father seemed to be rolling the word over in his mouth, as if tasting an unusual morsel. "Justice. Hrm. I cannot give you justice, my daughter. I may be able to offer you some completion."

"What do you mean?"

He pulled his pocket watch out of his trouser pocket, glanced at it, then at his daughter. "Come. Let's go to this courthouse then, and maybe you'll understand when you see."

"Thank you, father."

"We'll take the long route, though. You and I both know the trial itself is show. Your closure will come afterwards."

"How?"

"Just look in the man's eyes, child. Watch them when he's close enough. You'll learn all you need to know when he meets your gaze."

The trial was letting out as father and daughter arrived in their carriage. The steps of the courthouse were crowded with journalists and the curious, all the way to Cemal's waiting carriage. Seeing it was a sure sign that he was found innocent of wrongdoing. Aldora knew that it would be so, but the proof was still a powerful blow.

Her father sat at a cafe table some yards away from the crowd. "This will be quite close enough, I should think."

"We'd be closer near his carriage."

"This will be near enough."

"And how am I to see his eyes from here? I'd never make it through the crowd."

Her father ordered a coffee from the nearby waiter. "Oh, look, he's coming out."

Ignoring her father's calm, Aldora stood and craned her neck, trying to get a look at Cemal as his bodyguards attempted to clear a path through the crowd. She moved to get a closer look, only to be stopped by her father's aged but iron-firm grip around her wrist.

"Let me go—"

"Patience, Aldora. A lady never rushes for an appointment—"

"—she waits for the appointment to come to her," Aldora finished, standing and watching from a distance.

Cemal had stopped to address the crowd, speaking loudly in Turkish.

"My people," her father translated, studying the cafe's menu. "Many of you are unsure as to my guilt or innocence. This lawful trial, presided over by wise and powerful men, is my vindication. I harbour no ill will towards my accusers, but will stop at nothing to ferret out the monarchists behind this plot to set the Empire against—"

"*Hain*!" There was a sudden commotion as a cloaked figure pushed her way out of the crowd with a scream. The cloak fell back as she evaded Cemal's startled guards, and Aldora recognised Safiyya as surely as she recognised the glint of the curved dagger in the woman's hand.

"Hain!" she shouted again, leaping past Cemal's last defences to plunge her knife into the startled man's chest, again and again. "*Hiçbir erkek bana kullanacak! Bir daha asla!*"

"Betrayer," her father translated conversationally, releasing his grip on his daughter's wrist. "No man will ever use me. Never again."

The crowd screamed and seemed to fall away from the spectacle even as his guards surged forward to restrain her, too late to save their charge.

Aldora rushed past the fleeing crowd towards the steps in time to see police and bodyguards hauling the valet away from the wreckage of a once beautiful man, his face and chest cut to ribbons by a scorned woman's dagger. She didn't look into his eyes as he lay there, bleeding and still. She looked instead into Safiyya's wide rage-filled ones instead.

And saw her reflection.

ABOUT THE AUTHOR

Even before he could write Michael Coorlim was filling up spiral notebooks with stories, picture books presented to his grandparents as gifts, and performing small plays with his younger cousins for relatives during holiday gatherings. This love of storytelling stayed with him as he grew older, slumbering like an unawakened beast, sending him strange and terrifying dreams during his adolescence.

Even when not writing he feasted on the words of authors like Kurt Vonnegut, Terry Pratchett, Douglas Adams, and Ray Bradbury, spending so much time reading from hidden books in the middle of his middle school classes that his grades began to suffer. He'd sneak home with books that his teachers never assigned, and gorge on their contents overnight, and return them stealthily the next day only to take another.

Though a prolific writer he found the prospect and process of traditional publication daunting, often preparing query letters and researching markets only to never get around to submitting any of his work. It wasn't until he reached his thirties that he took the steps to write professionally, and by then the self-publishing revolution had already begun.

Michael currently lives in the city of Chicago with his girlfriend and their cat, living his childhood dream of supporting himself as an author of fast-paced character-driven fiction about authentic people in fascinating situations.

Printed in Germany
by Amazon Distribution
GmbH, Leipzig